LOVE AND HORROR

Gothic Classics

LOVE AND HORROR;

AN IMITATION OF THE PRESENT,

AND

A MODEL FOR ALL FUTURE

Romances.

BY

IRCASTRENSIS.

Edited with an Introduction and Notes by
Natalie Neill

Kansas City:
VALANCOURT BOOKS
2008

Love and Horror by Ircastrensis
First published in 1812
First Valancourt Books edition 2008

This edition © 2008 by Valancourt Books
Introduction and notes © 2008 by Natalie Neill

Library of Congress Cataloging-in-Publication Data

Ircastrensis
Love and horror : an imitation of the present, and a model for all future romances / by Ircastrensis ; edited with an introduction and notes by Natalie Neill.
p. cm. – (Gothic classics)
Includes bibliographical references.
ISBN 1-934555-44-4 (alk. paper)
1. Parody. I. Neill, Natalie, 1974- II. Title.
PR4821.I3L68 2008
823'.7–DC22

2008006069

Published by Valancourt Books
Kansas City, Missouri

Composition by James D. Jenkins
Set in Dante MT

10 9 8 7 6 5 4 3 2 1

CONTENTS

INTRODUCTION

By the time Jane Austen penned her Gothic parody *Northanger Abbey* (first version completed 1798; published 1818), it was commonplace for book reviewers to complain about "the trash with which the press now groans" (Austen 60). Literary critics in the late eighteenth and early nineteenth centuries frequently used metaphors of proliferation ("trash," "flood," "deluge," "fungous growth") to describe the period's burgeoning market for fiction. The type of novel most popular with Romantic-period reading audiences, Gothic, was also most subject to the critics' negative cant. Gothic was attacked both as a style of writing and a literary fashion. It was criticized in reviews, literary essays, and polemical texts for its narrative and stylistic excesses and supposed adverse effects on susceptible readers. Reaction against the genre also found expression in fiction: *Northanger Abbey*, Eaton Stannard Barrett's *The Heroine* (1813), and Thomas Love Peacock's *Nightmare Abbey* (1818) are just three of the better-known examples of a large body of parodic writing that emerged in response to first-wave Gothic.

The ostensible aim of the parodies was to laugh Gothic into extinction. There was a sense among critics, though, that the death of Gothic was already foretold in the Gothic novels themselves. The anonymous author of the anti-Gothic essay "Terrorist Novel Writing" (1797) remarked, for example: "Every absurdity has an end and as I observe that almost all novels are of the terrific cast, I hope the insipid repetition of the same bugbears will at length work a cure" (225). Similarly, Samuel Taylor Coleridge, in his 1797 review of Matthew Lewis's scandalous *The Monk* (1796), predicted that the reading public's taste for supernaturalism would be short-lived and that "ghosts and goblins" would soon "be found only in the lumber-garret of a circulating library" (197).

Gothic's longevity as a genre belies all predictions of its early demise. What is more, the Gothic novels of Ann Radcliffe, Lewis, and other Romantic-period authors have won wider reading audiences in recent decades than ever before. Yet Coleridge's prediction was accurate to the extent that many of the minor Gothic works of his age enjoyed fleeting popularity only to fade into obscurity. And, not surprisingly, the Gothic parodies of the period proved even more ephemeral than their targets. Although those by Austen, Barrett, and Peacock are still known today, most other early parodies of Gothic now go unread except by scholars and enthusiasts. Examples of these forgotten comic works include *Powis Castle: or, Anecdotes of an Antient Family* (1788), Henry James Pye's *The Spectre* (1789), James Cobb's *The Haunted Tower: A Comic Opera* (1789), William Beckford's *Modern Novel Writing* (1796) and *Azemia* (1797), R. S.'s *The New Monk* (1798),[1] F. C. Patrick's *More Ghosts!* (1798), Eliza Parsons's *Anecdotes of Two Well-Known Families* (1798), Mary Charlton's *Rosella, or, Modern Occurrences* (1799), Edward Du Bois's *St. Godwin: A Tale of the Sixteenth, Seventeenth, and Eighteenth Centuries* (1800), Thomas Disbin's *Bonifacio and Bridgetina* (1808), Dennis Lawler's *The Earls of Hammersmith; or, The Cellar Spectre* (1811), *Hardenbrass and Haverill; or, The Secret of the Castle* (1817), and Bellin de la Liborlière's *The Hero; or, The Adventures of a Night* (English edition, 1817).

Among the parodies of the Romantic period that deserve to be reprinted and rediscovered by twenty-first century readers is *Love and Horror* (1812) by "Ircastrensis." That Ircastrensis's Gothic spoof was at least moderately successful in its day is indicated by the fact that three years after its initial publication, a second edition appeared. Following the publication of the 1815 edition, however, the work sank into oblivion. Today the few surviving copies of the early texts lie mouldering into dust, not in lumber-garrets, but in rare

---

[1] In 2007, Valancourt Books published an edition of *The New Monk*, edited by Elizabeth Andrews.

book collections. The present edition, the first in more than 180 years, is thus an act of literary recovery—an attempt to reanimate an amusing ghost, which receded long ago into the shadows of literary history.

Ircastrensis wrote at least two works besides *Love and Horror*: the first was a travel narrative, *A Short Excursion in France* (1814), and the second, a novel, *The Annals of Orlingbury* (1815). Otherwise, little is known about the author, except what can be gleaned from his writing. Frederick S. Frank surmises that the pseudonym Ircastrensis may be "a compound of the Latin 'ire' or anger and 'castrametari,' or 'castrametation,' the term for the construction of a defensive military encampment of the legion on campaign." The pen name "then explains itself," he argues, "as 'angry defensive position against' all forms of Gothic flummery" (Frank 300n20). This theory reflects the military themes of *Love and Horror*, specifically the work's fictionalization of Peninsular War events and personages. Yet Ircastrensis's treatment of Gothic is not as scathing as Frank's interpretation of his name would suggest. The humour in the work is silly rather than caustic. It demonstrates the author's appreciation of the comic potential of Gothic devices and situations, as well as his keen sense of the ludicrous. But while the novel draws attention to the absurdities of Gothic, it also betrays an "ambivalent dependence" (Rosc 34) upon the genre. *Love and Horror* relies upon readers' familiarity with Gothic narratives for its comic effects. In this sense, it capitalizes upon the success of its targets. If Ircastrensis pokes fun at Gothic, he also satisfies readers' taste for Gothic excess. As is the case with many Gothic parodies, *Love and Horror* seems to address itself as much to fans as to detractors of the genre. Indeed, as Avril Horner and Sue Zlosnik have argued persuasively, comic Gothic works should be considered a form of Gothic literature in their own right and not merely "parasitic upon [...] serious Gothic writing" (Horner and Zlosnik 2000: 242).

Although *Love and Horror* may reveal the author's enjoyment of "serious" Gothic and his wish to exploit its popularity, these factors should not obscure the critical dimension of the work. For no less than the reviews and polemical essays of the Romantic period, Gothic parody was a site of literary criticism. Romantic-era parodists imitated Gothic in order to critique it from within. And by satirizing Gothic, and other popular fictional forms, they explored the limitations and potentials of literary discourse at a key moment in the development of the British novel.

Love and Horror employs the mock-heroic mode in order to satirize Gothic, which explains the author's decision to adopt a Latinate pen name. The subtitle of the second edition ("An Imitation of the Present, and a Model for all Future Romances") and prefatory remarks make it apparent from the outset that the novel is a high burlesque of Gothic romance. Ironic comparison is made in the Preface between contemporary Gothic novels and the classics, the tongue-in-cheek suggestion being that popular Gothic fiction is as worthy of emulation as the works of Homer and Virgil and the orations of Demosthenes and Cicero. In the narrative itself, much of the humour arises from the narrator's lofty treatment of Gothic clichés and character types. Allusions to famous epics and tragedies serve to contrast the protagonists of the novel, Annabella Tit and Thomas Bailey, with such figures as Hamlet, Lycidas, Aeneas, Dido, and Eloisa and Abelard. Epic conventions are also invoked in the service of Gothic parody. When the heroine Annabella happens upon a group of 500 robbers in a dark cavern, for example, the narrator calls upon the muses for inspiration: "Ye powers, who teach us what people think and say to themselves," he declares, "assist me in these and similar descriptions!" Of course, far from having an elevating effect, such displays of enthusiasm on the part of the narrator only accentuate the silliness of the plot and the excesses of Gothic narrative.

In the Preface, a joking reference to the "inimitable excellence" of contemporary literature highlights one of the most frequent criticisms levelled against early Gothic novels: namely, their lack of originality. Critics disparaged Gothic narratives for being formulaic and predictable. As Coleridge commented, "the public will learn, by the multitude of the manufacturers, with how little expense of thought or imagination this species of composition is manufactured" (296). The convoluted plot of *Love and Horror* incorporates, but rewrites in a comic register, nearly every defining element of first-wave Gothic, including a mysterious old portrait, providential meetings, uncertainty surrounding the birth of the hero and heroine, parental tyranny, a nefarious villain, ghosts, prophetic dreams, subterranean passageways, trap doors and magic springs, secret caverns, robbers, ruins, imprisonment, narrow escapes, and disguises. Through its *reductio ad absurdum* of Gothic conventions, *Love and Horror* mocks the derivative character of the mass-market Gothic fiction of its day. It is the novelistic equivalent to the shorter "recipes" for novel writing that were a popular form of verse parody during the Romantic period. One such poem is Mary Alcock's "A Receipt for Writing a Novel" (1799). Another quaint example, still sometimes quoted today, appeared in "Terrorist Novel Writing":

> *Take*—An old castle, half of it ruinous.
> A long gallery, with a great many doors, some secret ones.
> Three murdered bodies, quite fresh.
> As many skeletons, in chests and presses.
> An old woman hanging by the neck; with her throat cut.
> Assassins and desperadoes, *quant. suff.*
> Noises, whispers, and groans, threescore at least.
> Mix them together, in the form of three volumes, to

be taken at any of the watering places, before going to
bed. (225)

In listing the "ingredients" of Gothic horror, the recipe
calls attention to one of the paradoxes of Gothic writing,
that is, its tendency to be highly conventional despite its
marvellous and occasionally lurid subject matter and pur-
ported aim of horrifying or terrifying readers. Ircastrensis's
Gothic pastiche similarly makes fun of Gothic novels both
for their predictability and for the wild improbability of
their plotlines. The author piles on tropes from Gothic fiction and takes already improbable elements to preposterous extremes. For example, Gothic writing abounds with
resourceful heroines, but there is no heroine before Annabella Tit who manages to escape her persecutor by disguis-
ing herself as a dog! By the same token, every Gothic castle
has at least one secret trap door; in *Love and Horror*, the land-
scape is overrun with them.

The parody not only mocks well-worn Gothic elements,
it also emphasizes Gothic's indebtedness to earlier forms
of fiction. We see this especially in the work's portrayal of
the hero and heroine, and the manner in which they vent
their exalted emotions through bouts of weeping, fainting,
and other displays of agitation. Annabella and Thomas are
shown to have great sympathy for one another from their
earliest encounter. Thomas's heart "throbbed with such
violence," upon meeting the fair stranger in the theatre,
"that it loosened the button of his exterior garment, and
the vestment fell back in graceful and melancholy folds on
his shoulder." The flowery and stilted diction that the narrator employs is key to the work's critique of contemporary
literature, for it stresses not only the artificiality of Gothic
writing but also the influence that the eighteenth-century
novel of sensibility exerted on the genre. The subtitle of the
1812 edition of *Love and Horror* was "A Modern Romance,"
but it would not have taken Ircastrensis's first readers very

long to discover the irony of the phrase. The work's parody of sensibility romance suggests that "modern" novels in 1812 were not "modern" at all, but rather that many writers of the day were merely redeploying hackneyed phraseology and tired romance conventions from an earlier school of fiction. By exaggerating the redundancies and excesses of the so-called modern romance, Ircastrensis and other literary satirists called for greater innovation in novel writing and paved the way for nineteenth-century realism.

If *Love and Horror* satirizes the sensibility romances of the previous century, it also makes fun of the romantic sensibilities of its own day. As is the case with Peacock's *Nightmare Abbey*, Ircastrensis's novel is a satire of Romanticism written at the height of the Romantic Age. It provides an excellent site, therefore, for exploring the contending discourses and cultural tensions of a period that we sometimes tend to conceive too narrowly. *Love and Horror* anticipated *Nightmare Abbey* by using humour to attack what Peacock would, in 1818, term the "morbidities of modern literature" (Peacock 2001: 152). The work also set precedents for Peacock's comic novel by emphasizing the influence of German literature and thought upon British Gothic writing and British Romanticism in general. *Love and Horror* sends up such novels as Goethe's *The Sorrows of Young Werther* (1774) and Schiller's *The Ghost-Seer* (1786-88), as well as other works of German Gothic fiction and philosophy. Thomas Bailey is not only a caricature of a "man of feeling"; as with Peacock's Shelleyan character Scythrop Glowry, he is a parody of a *Sturm und Drang* hero. His apparent predilection for German metaphysics also makes him a precursor to the Coleridge figure in *Nightmare Abbey*, Mr. Flosky. Ircastrensis's satire of romantic transcendentalism is as comical as that found in Peacock's later work. For instance, near the beginning of *Love and Horror*, Thomas falls in love with a painting of a beautiful and mysterious woman. As he gazes at the portrait, he screams philosophically:

'Why [...] do I delay in this terrestrial, pendent, ever-whirling globe! Perhaps, as a disembodied tenant of the body, I might glide with her on the silent moon-beam, hang in mist over the river, or in the shape of beetles, tune together our harmonious twang, while flitting in the nocturnal ray of Sirius or Orion.'

When the narrator later refers to Thomas as being, "like many modern philosophers, fond of breathing gas through a tube," the reference is to the famous nitrous oxide experiments of 1799 in which Coleridge participated, a detail that suggests Ircastrensis had the poet-philosopher in mind when he wrote his satire.

After their initial meeting, Annabella and Thomas spend little time together, with the exception of a few brief and affecting reunions. The chapters alternate between their respective adventures so that the reader is often left in doubt about the fate of one character as the story follows the actions of the other. This shifting back and forth from one lover's story to the other's is a comic exaggeration of a storytelling technique Gothic writers employed to create and maintain suspense; however, it also works here precisely because Annabella and Thomas appear, at times, to occupy different diegetic worlds. Thomas's adventures are borrowed from the pages of German literature and military histories. The early part of the novel focuses on his melancholy temperament and ability to withstand horrors even more shocking than those depicted in German *Schauerromane* ("shudder novels"). In later chapters, he interacts with fictionalized versions of actual historical figures and performs impossible military feats. According to Ircastrensis's "secret history," it is Thomas Bailey, and not the Duke of Wellington, who is the true hero of the Napoleonic Wars. Annabella Tit's adventures, on the other hand, often appear to have been modelled upon those found in the so-called "female" Gothic romances of Ann Radcliffe and Regina Maria Roche (among others). Ircastrensis targets the highly accomplished female protagonists of Radcliffean Gothic in particular by demonstrating Annabella's extraordinary musical and artistic talents, and her penchant for extemporaneous artistic expression. Annabella's finely tuned sensibility parodies the characteristic sensitivity and emotional depth of Radcliffe's heroines, while her sometimes questionable sense of morality mocks their exemplary virtuousness. Not surprisingly, Ircastrensis takes his caricature of idealized femininity to ridiculous extremes. It was not unheard of for the gentle and susceptible heroines of Gothic romance to commune with animals: both Adeline, in Radcliffe's *Romance of the Forest* (1791), and Sibella Valmont, in Eliza Fenwick's *Secresy* (1795), have favourite pet fawns. Ircastrensis's heroine also acquires a little pet, but as the reader shall see, it is an altogether different sort of creature.

Near the end of *Northanger Abbey*, Catherine Morland realizes that the kinds of adventures depicted in her favourite Gothic novels ought not to be "looked for" in "the midland counties of England" at the turn of the nineteenth century (Austen 196). In *The Heroine*, Barrett similarly adopts a modern domestic setting in order to contrast the fantastic world of Gothic romance with the actual world of nineteenth-century England. The teenaged Cherry Wilkinson, fancying herself a heroine, runs away to London in search of her true birthright. After a series of pseudo-Gothic misadventures, however, she realizes the folly of her ways, gives up her books, and marries the levelheaded hero, Robert Stuart. Ircastrensis's parodic strategy also entails updating and domesticating Gothic romance. Thomas is the son of a butcher; Annabella, the daughter of a greengrocer. The first half of the novel is set in the busy market town where they live, and it is there, and not in some remote medieval castle, that many of their adventures occur. It is clear from the outset that Thomas and Annabella consider the duties of everyday life to be beneath them and, as with Cherry, they soon find their sense of superiority to their circumstances confirmed by the fortuitous "discovery" of aristocratic ties. The device parodies a plot pattern found in many Gothic romances, whereby the heroine (or hero) rises from a position of relative obscurity to great social heights, either by discovering high connections or by marrying well (often both). By counterposing the lofty expectations of the hero and heroine with a more prosaic reality, Ircastrensis heightens the absurdity of his Gothic story. Even in the midst of Annabella and Thomas's extraordinary adventures there are persistent reminders of mundane reality: an ancient relative includes in her prophecy tips on "restoring the colour of faded silks," and the solicitous narrator expresses concern that Annabella might catch a cold if she pauses too long in the subterranean passageway. Such bathetic contrasts produce humour and throw into relief Gothic's lack of realism.

Following in the anti-romance tradition of Cervantes's *Don Quixote* (1615) and Charlotte Lennox's *The Female Quixote* (1752), Annabella and Thomas are comic overreachers. But unlike such "Gothic Quixotes" as Catherine Morland and Cherry Wilkinson, Ircastrensis's hero and heroine are not disabused of their fancies at the narrative's conclusion. There is no attempt to impose a realistic ending by attributing all to the overactive imaginations of the protagonists. Instead, the narrative becomes more far-fetched as it advances. Annabella's claim to be the descendant of "Nicholas Tit, Lord" goes unchallenged; Thomas leads the Spanish Revolt. The preposterous incidents depicted in *Love and Horror* rival those found in even the most extravagant Gothic novels. Ircastrensis offers a critique of the improbabilities of Gothic romance; however, his parody is itself a rollicking work of imaginative fiction. And it is up to the reader either to enjoy the madness or throw down the book and declare, with one early nineteenth-century reviewer, "But enough of this trifling" (rev. of *Love and Horror*, "British Critic," 105).

It is not difficult to understand why Ircastrensis's novel

has been out of print for so long. The comic Gothic works peculiar to the Romantic period declined with the popularity of first-wave Gothic. In the years following the initial publication of *Love and Horror*, new forms of Gothic writing emerged to supplant the kinds of fictions that Ircastrensis had had in mind when he wrote his spoof. The parody not only targets a body of Gothic literature that is no longer as familiar as it once was, it is also sprinkled with topical references to Regency culture and politics, which create a dating and distancing effect. But *Love and Horror* has interest and value for precisely these reasons. When it was first published, critics may have dismissed it as an amusing *"bagatelle"* (rev. of *Love and Horror*, "British Critic," 104), but today it provides curious insight into the literary, social, and political worlds of early nineteenth-century England. Ircastrensis's work helps broaden the definition of Gothic literature and challenge notions of a monolithic Romantic culture. It also reminds us that such works as *Northanger Abbey* and *Nightmare Abbey* should not be read as isolated responses to Gothic, for they are in fact part of a much larger response by Romantic writers to the period's popular tales of "love and horror."

NATALIE NEILL
Toronto

April 14, 2008

ABOUT THE EDITOR

Natalie Neill is a Ph.D. candidate at York University researching Romantic and Victorian literature and culture. Her dissertation examines the relationship between Gothic parody and the development of novelistic discourse.

Works Cited

Alcock, Mary. "A Receipt for Writing a Novel." *Poems, &c. &c. by the Late Mrs. Mary Alcock.* London: C. Dilly, 1799. 89-93.

Austen, Jane. *Northanger Abbey.* 1818. Ed. Claire Grogan. Peterborough, Ontario: Broadview, 2002.

[Bellin de la Liborlière, Louis François Marie]. *The Hero; or, The Adventures of a Night: A Romance.* [Trans. Sophia Shedden]. Philadelphia: M. Carey & Son, 1817.

[Coleridge, Samuel Taylor.] Rev. of *The Monk*, by M. G. Lewis. *Critical Review* 19 (1797): 194-200.

Frank, Frederick S. "Gothic Gold: The Sadleir-Black Collection of Gothic Fiction." *Studies in Eighteenth-Century Culture* 26 (1998): 287-312.

Horner, Avril and Sue Zlosnik. "Comic Gothic." *A Companion to the Gothic.* Ed. David Punter. Oxford: Blackwell, 2000. 242-254.

Rev. of *Love and Horror; an Imitation of the Present and a Model for all Future Romances*, by Ircastrensis. *British Critic, New Series* Vol. 5. London: F. C. and J. Rivington, 1816. 104-105.

"The Mermaid," *The Mirror of Literature, Amusement, and Instruction.* 1.3 (1822): 35-38.

Peacock, Thomas Love. *The Letters of Thomas Love Peacock.* Vol. 1. Ed. Nicholas A. Joukovsky. Oxford: Claredon, 2001.

———. *Nightmare Abbey / Crotchet Castle.* 1818/1831. London: Penguin, 1986.

Rose, A. Margaret. *Parody/Meta-Fiction.* London: Croom Helm, 1979.

Schiller, Friedrich. *The Armenian; or, The Ghost Seer.* Vol. 1. Trans. W[ilhelm] Render. London: C. Whittingham for H. D. Symonds, 1800.

"Terrorist Novel Writing" in *The Spirit of the Public Journals for 1797.* Vol. 1. 2nd ed. London: James Ridgway, 1799. 223-225.

Suggestions for Further Reading

Clery, E. J. and Robert Miles. "Anti-Gothic" in *Gothic Documents: A Sourcebook, 1700-1820*. Manchester and New York: Manchester University Press, 2000. 173-222.

Gaull, Marilyn. "Romantic Humor: The Horse of Knowledge and the Learned Pig." *Mosaic* 9.4 (1976): 43-63.

Horner, Avril and Sue Zlosnik. *Gothic and the Comic Turn*. Basingstoke: Palgrave Macmillan, 2005.

Jones, Daryl. "Gothic Parody." *The Handbook to Gothic Literature*. Ed. Marie Mulvey-Roberts. Basingstoke: Palgrave Macmillan, 1998. 270-271.

Jones, Steven E. *Satire and Romanticism*. New York: St. Martin's, 2000.

———., ed. *The Satiric Eye: Forms of Satire in the Romantic Period*. New York: Palgrave Macmillan, 2003.

Kelly, Gary. "Unbecoming a Heroine: Novel Reading, Romanticism, and Barrett's *The Heroine*" in *Nineteenth-Century Literature* 45.2 (1990): 220-241.

Kent, David A. and D. R. Ewen, eds., *Romantic Parodies*. Foreword by Linda Hutcheon. Rutherford, N.J.: Fairleigh Dickinson University Press, 1992.

Lau, Beth. "Madeline at *Northanger Abbey*: Keats's Anti-Romances and Gothic Parody," *JEGP* 84 (1985): 30-50.

Lewis, Paul. "Humor and Fear in the Gothic" in *Comic Effects: Interdisciplinary Approaches to Humor in Literature*. Albany: SUNY Press, 1989. 111-153.

———. "Gothic and Mock Gothic: The Repudiation of Fantasy in Barrett's *The Heroine*." *English Language Notes* 21.1 (1983): 44-52.

May, Leland Chandler. *Parodies of the Gothic Novel*. New York: Arno, 1980.

Milbank, Alison. "Gothic Satires, Histories and Chap-Books." *Gothic Fiction: Rare Printed Works from the Sadleir-Black Collection of Gothic Fiction at the Alderman*

Library, University of Virginia: A Listing and Guide to the Microfilm Collection. Ed. Peter Otto, Alison Milbank, and Marie Mulvey-Roberts. Marlborough: Adam Matthew, 2003. 61-79.

Norton, Rictor, ed. "Parody" in *Gothic Readings: The First Wave, 1764-1840.* London and New York: Leicester University Press, 2000. 259-278.

Renier, Anne. "Love and Horror." *The Private Library: The Quarterly Journal of the Private Libraries Association* 3.5 (1961): 60-63.

Sage, Victor. "Gothic Laughter: Farce and Horror in Five Texts." *Gothick Origins and Innovations.* Ed. Allan Lloyd-Smith and Victor Sage. Amsterdam: Rodopi, 1994.

Stones, Graeme, and John Strachan, eds. *Parodies of the Romantic Age: The Poetry of the Anti-Jacobin and Other Parodic Writings.* 5 vols. London: Pickering & Chatto, 1998.

Weiss, Fredric. *The Antic Spectre: Satire in Early Gothic Novels.* New York: Arno, 1980.

A Note on the Text

The first edition of *Love and Horror* was printed in London in 1812 by T. Bensley. A subsequent edition, published by Stockdale, appeared in 1815. The present edition is based on the 1815 text. Spelling, syntax, and punctuation have been left untouched, except in places where an error was apparent or where I thought that a slight alteration might help to dispel confusion. In general, the text has been edited lightly. Peculiarities in language are not only key to Ircastrensis's parody of Gothic writing, they also contribute to the humour and charm of the work.

I am grateful to the Rare Books Librarians at the Albert and Shirley Small Special Collections Library at the University of Virginia, where one of the few extant copies of *Love and Horror* is housed. They were welcoming and helpful both times I visited the library (first to read and then to transcribe the work). I would also like to thank Cristina Favretto, a Rare Books Librarian at the Charles E. Young Research Library, at UCLA, who kindly sent me a copy of the Preface to the first edition of *Love and Horror* (it did not, however, differ materially from the 1815 Preface). A special thank you to Paul Cnudde, Kim Michasiw, Lesley Higgins, Ian Balfour, Sharon Neill, and Robin Neill for their generous and insightful advice at different stages of the project.

L O V E

H O R R O R;

AN IMITATION OF THE PRESENT,

AND

A MODEL FOR ALL FUTURE

Romances.

~~~~~~~~~~~~~~~~~~~~~~~

BY IRCASTRENSIS ;

Author of A short Excursion in France, and Annals of
Orlingbury, a Novel.

~~~~~~~~~~~~~~~~~~~~~~~

PRINTED FOR J. J. STOCKDALE, 41, PALL MALL.

1815.

Facsimile of the title page of the second edition (1815)
(Reproduced from the best available copy.)

Love and Horror

DEDICATION.

I SHOULD have wished to dedicate this little Book to a Noble Family, with which I have been connected for some time, whose uniformly steady, liberal, and enlightened conduct I can never sufficiently admire. But the thing is not worthy of them. If, however, this Work should meet their eye, and they should discover the Author, I beg them to accept it as a private mark of gratitude and affection.

PREFACE.

A REGULAR imitation of the sublime models of the present day certainly requires some apology; the public have a right to demand it, and the character of the imitator will rather gain by the concession. It may be contended that if former writers have attained perfection, there can be but little use in further efforts. There is an innate lurking vicinity in the minds of men that forbids them to yield tamely to such reasonings. No man ever handles the pen, the chisel, or the pencil, without some latent hope of excelling those who have gone before him. Though I may not attain their general excellence, there may be particulars possibly in which, to speak modestly, I have somewhat gone beyond the efforts of former writers. It would be a bad world for us artists, if we should suffer ourselves to be deterred by even inimitable excellence. In fact, we have never yielded to it; many orators have been found on their legs since the days of Cicero and Demosthenes; epic poems have been written since Homer; and, after the numerous romances of the present century, "Love and Horror" makes its appearance, to close the procession, and add one ridge to the long Appennines.

LOVE AND HORROR.

CHAPTER I.

THE storm was beating tempestuously, and the lightning glaring around the playhouse at E——,* when Mr. Thomas Bailey was walking along in deep meditation by the door. The lights, the company, the noise, and the crowd, at last roused him from his torpor; and throwing down the stipulated price with a contemptuous smile at the sordid avarice of his fellow creatures, who would not afford even amusements for nothing, "Happy are the birds," exclaimed he to himself, pausing on every step as he entered the interior of the building; "happy are beetles, wasps, muck-flies, they know nothing of the miseries of human nature, which have encumbered, encumber, and will for ever encumber, in their direst shape, the agitated and hapless form of Mr. Thomas Bailey." Those who stood around the entrance of the pit, observing his melancholy and frenzied aspect, in silent respect to his feelings made way for his gliding form, which soon insinuated itself into the middle of a nearly empty pit. Mr. Thomas Bailey sat down in the most intense abstraction: the shouting multitudes around him, the sounding forms of fiddles, had no effect on him; like a leaden statue, or a Caucasean rock,* he stood unmoved in his own sorrows. The surrounding company gave him no sensations but that of being in a desert, in a state of the most awful and contemplative solitude. "These crowds," exclaimed he in a voice of horror to himself, "have no sympathy with me; their futile and inane minds are taken up with vain sounds, absorbed in the view of fabled theatric pains; they have no leisure for the contemplation of their own sorrows; perhaps, O agonizing thought! not a single mind, nor even half a mind, is occupied with my image. If Mr. Thomas Bailey were at this very moment being wrecked on the shores of the Bosphorus, were his pendent form wrapped about in sheeted lightning, and blown by the polar winds, these personages would, in all probability, relax not the least tittle of their amusement." Heart-rending thought! he could no longer endure it, when nature came to his relief in a shower of pearly tears. He might have continued in this state of feeling during the whole of the representation, if his attention had not been arrested by a muffled female form close at his elbow. Whenever Thomas lifted up his handkerchief to his eyes, the muffled female form lifted up a similar implement to her countenance; when Thomas sighed, the unknown fair one re-echoed sigh for sigh; when Thomas uttered a stifled groan, the interesting stranger replied with a stifled groan; but in so tender, graceful, and dignified a manner, as fully shewed the utterer to be in possession of every virtue and every beauty under heaven. No common soul could have given birth to a groan of such import; it spoke volumes. The heart of Thomas throbbed with such violence, that it loosened the button of his exterior garment, and the vestment fell back in graceful and melancholy folds on his shoulder. The stranger gave a gratuitous and heart-piercing sigh. Thomas glanced his eyes over her form, which was so enveloped in veils and cloaks, that he could form no conclusion whether he had or had not ever before seen the interesting and all-amiable stranger. "You sympathize with me," said he, in the softest and most persuasive manner. "I do indeed," said she, in a most graceful whisper. "Alas," sighed Thomas, "my widowed heart will never be the receptacle of the least grain of joyous sentiment." "Widowed!" re-sighed the stranger; "how long?" Thomas looked wildly about the playhouse, from the pit to the gallery; from the gallery to the pit, then to the gallery again, in ceaseless succession. "The loss must have been recent," said the stranger; "how long have you lost your love?" "Two hundred years ago," mysteriously sighed Thomas.

CHAPTER II.

IN order to account for the deep sorrows of Mr. Thomas Bailey, it will be necessary to look back about a year before the commencement of this history. Before this he was remarkable for the easy flow of his spirits, and his graceful as well as majestic demeanour. In the exercises of his youth, in the sprightly and harmonious dance, in venatorial exercitations,* none exceeded, and few, very few indeed, equalled Mr. Thomas Bailey. On a sudden, one Friday morning, his looks and demeanour suddenly altered; his step became slow and melancholy, though still graceful and majestic; his voice became low and inharmonious; his coat became spotted and threadbare; and his spirits were so much reduced, that he cared neither to buy a new coat, nor to re-brush the old one. The cause of all this was as follows. It happened on a Thursday as the form of Mr. Thomas Bailey was gliding down a back lane of the city, that he saw a crowd of persons collected about a door. He inquired, in the sweetest tones and in the most winning manner, what was the occasion of that congregation. The person to whom he addressed himself, bowing gracefully, informed him that there was a sale of pictures within. Thomas smiled his thanks; and, little thinking what the harsh fates intended for him, sprung with alacrity into the house. A picture of a lady was at that very moment being exposed for sale; it was painted on a large canvas, and without a frame, and time had worn many holes in the superficies; but in the countenance he discerned so

much sympathy, and the eyes seemed to be turned to him
with such languishing sweetness, that he immediately concluded that the original of this picture must be the person
to whom the fates intended to unite the frame of Thomas.
Under this impression he turned first pale, then red, then
pale again; various agitations unfelt before pervaded the
form of Thomas. He was unable to stand; and, leaning on
the person who stood next to him, he wiped the livid drops
from his agonizing brow. It was a severe crisis for Thomas.
In the mean time two or three persons were bidding for
the picture. As they had no sympathy with the picture, they
urged the matter languidly; but Thomas proceeded with
agitation and emotion. The personage selling the pictures,
perceiving his emotion, artfully played with it, and the picture at length became the property of Thomas at double
the value of it. Beckoning to a menial who attended the
house, he departed with the picture to the mansion of his
father, the venerable Jeremiah Bailey. He carried it himself
up stairs, and deposited it in his bed-room, by his dressing
table. He took sufficient nutriment with him, and appeared
no more that evening to the eyes of his expecting family.
Placing a chair opposite to the picture, he sat for hours contemplating its many beauties and virtues; at last starting up,
and bestowing on its lips a burning kiss, he exclaimed, "By
the blood of all the Baileys, none but thy resemblance shall
ever be the co-mate of Thomas. Would to heaven I knew
where to find thee! Wert thou dwelling in the most distant
island, where no ship could come, my gliding form should
dash through the waves, and present to thy eyes the ardent
and impetuous form of the lover of . . . . . . of whom?" added
he, in a voice of despair, at the same time smiting his head
with a poker that accidentally stood near him. To resolve
his doubts he examined the back of the picture, and found
written there the name of Ethelinda, joined to a date above
two hundred years ago. The knowledge of this horrid truth

was too much for the frame of Thomas; his knees knocked against each other, the blood forsook his cheeks, respiration ceased, and the son of Jeremiah fell senseless in the chair!

CHAPTER III.

IN this deplorable state was Thomas found on the Friday morning by Imogene, a female menial of the mansion, in her daily visit to the different apartments. Horror seized her at the sight; for she thought at first that the spirit of the lover of Ethelinda had deserted its mortal receptacle. Unwilling to trouble Jeremiah, who was always particularly cross if interrupted at breakfast time, she determined to ascertain, by every experiment in her power, whether he was or was not among the dead. She held a mirror to his mouth, and had the pleasure to see it instantly soiled by the breath of Thomas. Immediately she warmed a spirituous cordial which she happened to have in her pocket, and applied it to the mouth of the son of Jeremiah. To her great delight he swallowed it, and gave signs of animation, if indeed the melancholy state he was in could be called animation; for his cheeks were pale, his eyes goggling, and his voice dull and cadaverous. He spoke but few words; and though almost hourly interrogated by his affectionate relatives, he maintained an intense silence on the secret subject of his mysterious sorrows. He discontinued his accustomed exercises, and rigidly abstained from all nourishment; so that he appeared but little different from a moving anatomy. "O, Ethelinda!" would he cry daily as he contemplated the picture: "if the inexorable fates have yet spared thee, how much must time have withered thy beauty! My Ethelinda will resemble the mowed flower, which in the morning was the glory of the field. Yet still, Ethelinda, still you will excel your sex as the dried rose leaf excels the living thistle. O,

Ethelinda!" screamed he, "living or dead, thou art destined
to be the ceaseless torment of thy Thomas! Why," says he,
"do I delay in this terrestrial, pendent, ever-whirling globe!
Perhaps, as a disembodied tenant of the body, I might glide
with her on the silent moon-beam, hang in mist over the
river, or in the shape of beetles, tune together our harmonious twang, while flitting in the nocturnal ray of Sirius or
Orion." At these words he lifted up the poker, and gave
himself several desperate raps on the forehead. It happened
that the inflictions gave the son of Jeremiah considerable
pain, and he stopped to rub the part with his hand, and to
apply a little brown paper, suffused in vinegar, to the spot.
In the mean time, the family, alarmed at the low and melancholy sounds which they heard, rushed together into the
room, and took possession of the poker. This opportune
arrival saved the life of Thomas; for otherwise he would
have begun again shortly in a fresh place, and his flitting
ghost would soon have found some little hole at which it
might have escaped. The family undressed the son of Jeremiah, and deposited his frame in a bed. They then gave him
a draught of warmed spirituous cordial, raised his head on
the pillow, and put into his hands the Whole Duty of Man;*
and, bowing gracefully, left him to his meditations. The son
of Jeremiah, wisely thinking that one attempt on his life was
enough for one hero, in the course of one day, sunk back
on his pillow, and enjoyed a sweet repose in the arms of the
brother of death. He was at length awakened by the fall of
the book on the floor; and, looking towards the picture, perceived that some of the family in gliding gracefully out of the
room, had carried it away with them. A proceeding of this
kind naturally threw Mr. Thomas Bailey into the deepest
despair. He was afraid that entreaties would be of no avail;
and to call in the civil authorities would at once wound the
heart of relatives formerly kind and considerate; and, at the
same time, expose his tender and never-to-be-obliterated

connexion with Ethelinda to the profane and unsentimental
vulgar. At all events, he perceived that a sword of division
had passed between himself and his family; and much as
his tender heart regretted it, yet stern necessity compelled
him to regard them as the worst of enemies. Through their
means he felt himself existing alone in the midst of infinite
space, and as fallen into a den of awful and unutterable solitude. The feeling was too much for Thomas. It seemed to
him that he could break and dash to pieces every article of
the furniture, fling tea cup against tea cup, mirror against
mirror, bason against ewer, and lastly, hew to pieces all the
chairs and tables, and sacrifice all his relatives to the tenth
degree, together with the pictures of all his ancestors; the
cat, the dog, the tame magpie, and the owl; and, finally, cut
his own throat. But in tossing about his hands, they accidentally touched his forehead; then he found with Clarence,
"What pain it was to die."* The thought was agonizing! he
dabbed* the cup which held the cordial on the floor; then
the snuffers, then the snuffer stand; tore an immense hole
in the curtains, bit the sheets in awful fury; then fell back on
his pillow in a livid and heart-rending swoon!

CHAPTER IV.

Though Thomas had in appearance sufficient cause to condemn his family for gliding gracefully out of the room with
his picture, yet had they innocently incurred his displeasure. They had no suspicion of his connexion with the lost
Ethlinda; and the cause of withdrawing it was as follows: an
Armenian merchant, who was present when the son of Jeremiah bought the picture, thought it would make a pretty
ornament to a palace he had in Armenia.* With this view he
determined to purchase it at any rate, and actually offered
to the father of Thomas ten times as much as the son of

Jeremiah had given for it. Jeremiah accepted the offer with joy, and with the money immediately satisfied the demands of the shoemaker of the lover of Ethelinda. Poor incongruous man! he thought his son would be rejoiced at being liberated from that implacable creditor. Rejoiced, indeed, at the loss of every thing that bound him to this sublunary vale. Rather let the personage rage insatiably through the streets of the city; rather let all the leather and the shoemakers in the world meet one common fate. As soon as Thomas had recovered from his swoon, he dressed himself; and, with a slow and majestic step, left the house. He had advanced as far as the great wall of the cathedral when he beheld two Armenians passing on in a slow procession with the picture of the lost Ethelinda. He immediately felled one of them to the earth; and was approaching to attack the other, when the Armenian touched a brass spring, and the wall of the cathedral opened.* He leaped immediately with the picture, dragging after him the body of his companion, and the wall closed on the astonished Thomas. An officer of the cathedral passing by at this moment, he questioned him about the mystery of the wall; but the officer, thinking the intellects of the son of Jeremiah disordered, left him abruptly, asking him with a bitter sneer, how he thought it possible for the wall of a cathedral to open by a brass spring. Thomas remained for a long time searching for the spring, but his search was in vain, for the Armenian had carried it with him. The fact is, that being an ingenious as well as a nefarious character, he had contrived this spring, so that he could open and instantly close any wall; by which means he often escaped the punishment due to his crimes. Thomas marched onward with the frenzied feelings of despair; and at the end of a solitary street he saw the Armenian walking by himself with the picture. The son of Jeremiah now determined to assert his rights to the lost Ethelinda. He advanced with the rapidity of irritated feelings. The Arme-

nian smiled contemptuously; and, when the son of Jeremiah
approached him, he stamped on the ground; a secret trap
door opened, and twenty Negroes ascending with drawn
swords and daggers, surrounded the Armenian. After standing a few minutes in a determined and menacing attitude,
they slowly and solemnly descended into the vault below.
The Armenian descended last; and, grinning horribly at
Thomas, so much incensed the lover of Ethelinda, that he
seized a spear that accidentally lay in the street; and, hurling
it at his antagonist, had the pleasure of seeing him fall with
a dreadful groan into the cavity, and the trap door closed
with a noise of thunder. Thomas examined every part of the
ground, and found it equally level, so artfully had the nefarious monster contrived this retreat. It was at this instant that
a tremendous storm of wind, rain, and lightning, drove the
unconscious form of Mr. Thomas Bailey towards the door
of the playhouse. The muffled female form concluded from
the answer of the son of Jeremiah that reason had deserted
its seat; but such was her respect and tender affection for the
form of Thomas, that she thought it better to be mad with
him than in her right senses with any body else. Influenced
by this tender sympathy, she unconsciously continued to
imitate every action of the son of Jeremiah; and gracefully
insinuating her toe over the foot of the lover of Ethelinda,
in order to shew the agonizing state of her mind, she made
many tender pressures on the toe of Thomas. The heart of
Thomas responded by an elevation of his toe, and this pen-
dulous movement produced as great a sympathy between
Thomas and the mysterious muffled form, as if he had lived
one hundred years alone with her on the top of a desert
mountain. The performance had passed unheeded by them,
and they were entirely unconscious where they were, till
roused to locality by the noise of the retreating spectators.
They instinctively glided through several streets; when, at
the corner of one of them, the mysterious female, over-

come by her sensations, threw her arms round his neck, and bestowed a burning kiss on the cheek of Thomas. With sympathetic fervour he withdrew her veil; when, to his infinite astonishment, by the glare of a neighbouring lamp, he discovered the face of Ethelinda!

CHAPTER V.

THOMAS was in the highest degree of rapture, and was about to testify his joy in a long speech, the loss of which the historian laments as the greatest calamity that ever befell him, when a terrific and austere form rushed between them; and, seizing Ethelinda by the arm, bore her away with the rapidity of the mountain torrent. Thomas was so much amazed, that he remained in stupid torpor, till the mysterious female form, with her mysterious ravisher, had passed the corner of a street, and had vanished. Thomas was not long at leisure to meditate on this calamity before he felt himself seized by four and twenty men, and hurried along with unceasing rapidity. At last the whole party stopped, and one of them rung a bell, the horrific and sullen tones of which the son of Jeremiah heard far under ground. At length a door opened, and the form of Mr. Thomas Bailey was dragged though several dark passages and winding staircases, till he was brought into the middle of a large subterraneous hall, fully lighted up, and having a table at the upper end covered with a black cloth, round which sat the forms of counsellors, and on a raised seat one dressed as a judge.* Thomas, in a firm and manly tone of voice, exclaimed, "Why am I brought here?" "We accuse you of murder, by the name of Mr. Thomas Bailey," uttered a low sepulchral voice under his feet. "Of whom?" said Thomas. "Of an Armenian merchant." Thomas trembled, and turned pale; for he knew too well the truth of the accusation. The judge said, "Since

we are all convinced that you are guilty, there is no need
for further trial. But as it fortunately happened, that the
person you intended to murder is still alive, though under
the hands of the apothecary, we shall have mercy on you;
and instead of commanding you to expire under the most
horrific torments, we merely order you to be drowned; and
let it be the care of the four and twenty lictors* that this
sentence be fully executed." The judges and the counsellors
vanished through separate doors, and the son of Jeremiah
was left in the hands of the lictors, who instantly prepared
to execute the sentence. They accordingly led Mr. Thomas
Bailey through the dark stairs and passages, till they came
to the open air. They carried with them a large weight of
iron, and a string to fasten it to the neck of Thomas. They
also provided long spears; that in case the form of Thomas
should emerge to the top of the water, they might poke
him down again. Then, in a slow and solemn procession,
they adjourned to a neighbouring pool. They then, that he
might have no cause of complaint, read to him the merciful
sentence of the judge; fastened the iron weight about his
neck; and, having surrounded the pool with their spears,
they jerked Thomas into the middle of the water, and the
son of Jeremiah sunk instantly to the bottom.

CHAPTER VI.

WE will now give some account of the muffled female form,
and explain the reason of her strange resemblance to Ethelinda, which, without some explanation, might seem a little
mysterious to the ordinary reader. We shall also explain
who the horrific and stern form was that hurried her away
so abruptly, with other particulars necessary to be known
respecting the lady; and, above all, that most mysterious
sympathy which she felt for the sorrows of Thomas. Know,

then, that she was not Ethelinda, neither had she been born
two hundred years ago; for; if so, she would not have been
much surprized at the answer of Thomas. She was in fact
a lineal descendant of Ethelinda, which accounts for the
seemingly astonishing resemblance she bore to the picture.
Her name was Miss Annabella Tit, the daughter of Mr.
Abraham Tit, a gentleman engaged in a mercantile capacity. The vulgar chose to call him a greengrocer; though,
as he often observed to me, he was neither green, nor a
grocer. His real appellation, he observed, should be Mr. Tit,
merchant, or Mr. merchant Tit. There were some mysteries about his descent which shall be revealed in due time.
The Tits, he would say, in former times—but we must be
silent for the present. There were many stern traits in the
character of Mr. Abraham Tit which often rendered him
very disagreeable to Annabella. His mind was not always
capable of being moved by high-wrought susceptibility. He
sometimes insisted on her performing offices by no means
consistent with the dignity of a heroine such as——but I will
not sully my pages by mentioning them. But the worst trait
of all was, his objecting to her innocent practice of walking
from midnight till three o'clock near an old ruined tower
in the neighbourhood.* I protest that I blush to the nib of
my pen while I recount these heart-rending instances of
parental austerity. Poor Annabella! ill-fated Tit! Abraham,
however, had at times some touch of human nature; and, as
fathers generally go, was by no means a bad one.

Annabella had long felt her heart enlivened by the flame
of love; but it was for an ideal object, a compound of all
the characters she had ever heard or read of. She thought it
impossible, for then she knew not Mr. Thomas Bailey, that
half the virtues and perfections she thought of could centre
in one human being. "Alas!" said she in an agony, "I must
have a dozen or a score lovers at once, if I wish to be sup-
plied with all the contradictory qualities I sigh for." While

Annabella was thus giving vent to her pure and tender emotions, without being at all aware of the existence of that epitome of all human perfection, Mr. Thomas Bailey, the son of Jeremiah continued, day after day, languishing before a picture, while the white hands of Annabella remained unpressed, and her ruby lips were of no use but as a thoroughfare for sighs, which issued forth to mingle with the midnight breeze. In a paroxysm of this kind she once sunk into a kind of disturbed sleep. She fancied that the awful and sainted shade of Ethelinda Tit, her great ancestor, approached her in a sad and solemn step, with a mournful waving of the head; and, after hearing the relation of her deep sorrows, and giving her many admonitions, together with many good receipts* for restoring the colour of faded silks, left her with this remarkable prophecy:

> Where mimic sorrows are dealt out for gold,
> There seek a lover, and a lover hold.

She at first thought this oracle alluded to the circulating library, where the librarian, for the sake of lucre, details the multifarious woes of heroes and heroines. But in her constant attendance at this spot she found none but heroines like herself, or those who, having outlived the age of heroinism, were desirous of living it over again in books. She then attended funerals, where sorrow is often mimic, but there she met with no better success. At last, when she almost despaired of happiness, as she was gliding by an old wall, her eye was struck by a notice for the representation of a new tragedy. Immediately she screamed out with Hamlet, "The play's the thing at which I'll catch." The sorrows of modern tragedy are often mimic; and, like most mimicries, bear generally but a ludicrous resemblance to the originals. Almost unconsciously she repeated the words of the prophecy:

Where mimic sorrows are dealt out for gold,
There seek a lover, and a lover hold.

It happened, unfortunately for this plan, that the form of
Abraham Tit, merchant, had very considerable objections
to theatrical representation. In the first place, it was a con-
sumption of money without any return; secondly, it consumed time which might be better employed; and thirdly,
it was too apt to set the imagination of the spectator agog.
Annabella consequently formed a design of visiting the
playhouse without the knowledge of her parent, Mr. Abraham Tit. But that sagacious parent, observing the extraordinary care she took to conceal her person, determined to
watch the glidings of her form. Accordingly, to his great
displeasure, he traced her to the playhouse, and returning
at the end of the performance, to his great amazement he
beheld her issue forth with the form of Mr. Thomas Bailey.
The parent of Annabella was a witness to their conversation, and heard that pure and burning kiss bestowed under
the lamp, on the cheek of Thomas. He could master his
irritated feelings no longer; but, rushing between them, he
hurried Annabella home, growling all the way like an Adri-
atic whirlwind, and immediately sent the friend of Thomas,
without supper, to her couch.

CHAPTER VII.

IT is now time to return to Thomas, whom we left at the
bottom of a pool, with a large weight round his neck, and
with no hope of life if he should rise to the top. The four
and twenty lictors after having staid half an hour near the
pool, and having seen nothing of Thomas, went away, concluding he was dead. They delivered in their report to the
judges and counsellors of the secret tribunal, that the son
of Jeremiah was numbered among the dead. It happened

however, fortunately for Mr. Thomas Bailey, that he was
an acute philosopher; and, like many modern philosophers,
fond of breathing gas through a tube.* For this purpose, he
was never without a bladder in his pocket filled with vital
air, and accommodated with a brass pipe, and a stop cock.
The obvious use of this struck the mind of Thomas in the
secret cavern, and he was secretly rejoiced at the sentence
of drowning, which he knew so well how to avoid. With
these thoughts he marched with such a firm and composed
step to the place of execution as astonished the lictors, and
drew admiration from those stern executioners of the law.
One of them was so much affected, that he shook the son
of Jeremiah by the hand at the edge of the pool, and offered
him part of a spirituous cordial, which Thomas gracefully
refused. As soon as the son of Jeremiah found himself at the
bottom of the pool, he seated himself on the weight; and
drawing the bladder from his pocket, began to suck the tube
with infinite contentment. When he heard the retreating
steps of the four and twenty lictors, he cut the string which
connected him with the weight, and rising to the top, he
soon gained the bank. In the distance he beheld the terrific
and shadowy forms of the lictors, and beheld the glittering
of their retreating spears. On his way home an awfully-muf-
fled personage crossed his path; and, at the sight of Thomas,
started with considerable signs of terror and alarm. The
son of Jeremiah immediately conjectured that it was either
the judge or one of the counsellors, or the hated head of
his Armenian enemy. The last guess was well founded; it
was indeed the Armenian; who, having partially recovered
from his wound, was proceeding to the execution of some
nefarious project. He had just come from the secret cavern,
where he had heard the death of Thomas solemnly attested
by the four and twenty lictors. This made him feel some
surprize and alarm at the sight of Thomas, whom he at first
imagined to be some disembodied tenant of the body. He

determined, however, to watch near his father's mansion. When Thomas approached the habitation of Jeremiah, he observed a glaring visage near the portal, which he immediately knew to be that of the Armenian. He felt alarmed at the danger of being again exposed to the machinations of the secret tribunal. The Armenian withdrew immediately in the greatest wrath against the four and twenty lictors, and drew up an accusation against them, which he immediately presented to the supreme judge of the secret tribunal. The judge smiled his assent, and immediately ordered four and twenty cups of poison to be presented to the four and twenty lictors. They bowed gracefully, drank the potion, and instantly expired. Their bodies were immediately, one by one, precipitated into a dark and deep vault under the hall of judgment.

CHAPTER VIII.

THE form of Thomas, without holding any communication with his apparently treacherous family, had glided silently into his bed-room, and retired to bed. Here he reflected on his awful situation; he was cut off entirely from the world, from society, and from his family, and menaced by dangers which he knew neither how to meet or avoid. Above, beneath, around, was infinite space, filled with planets and stars. Thomas was puzzled, in the highest degree, about the ring of Saturn, and the belts of Jupiter; his thoughts flew from the moon to the comet,* from the comet to the moon; the whirl of his ideas was agonizing; he fell back on his pillow exhausted. "O solitude, solitude," screamed he, "I begin to know what thou art. O ye planets, comets, stars, satellites, is there any body in your glittering frames who sympathizes with Thomas?" Having said this he fell into an uneasy ephialtic sleep,* from which he was shortly awakened by a slight buzz. It was not without a certain degree of astonishment that he beheld the pallid forms of the four and twenty lictors around his bed. "Well, sirs," cried Thomas, "what is your pleasure now?"

"O Thomas, Thomas," cried the lictor,
"'Tis you who are at last the victor."

"My very good and ingenious sir," cried Thomas, "I perceive that two brothers are waiting for my embraces, death and sleep. To whichever of these you dismiss me, do it in plain prose, I am not in a humour to be joked with." "O son of Jeremiah!" cried the lictors, "you mistake us, we are thy friends." "Friends!" said Thomas, his heart expanding at the words: "Friends! oh, oh!" "Look here," cried they in a low sepulchral tone of voice; "look here!" said they, mourningly waving a cup in each of their hands, "we are poisoned on account of thee: join us in revenge against the secret judge, and his secret counsellors: we will visit thee often." "At your leisure, gentlemen," said Thomas; "at present I am indisposed and sleepy:" so saying, he turned his head from them; and the lictors after having given him a sign by which he might call them at anytime, instantly vanished. Thomas had sunk a second time into an uneasy slumber, when he was awakened by a slight motion of the curtain. "What!" cried he, "are you returned so soon?" He turned around with impatience to chide the lictors for their importunity, when he beheld the Armenian standing over him with a drawn dagger!

CHAPTER IX.

IT will not be improper to return to Annabella, who was lying awake in her bed at midnight, painfully lamenting to herself the unaccountable brutality of her father, Mr. Abraham Tit, merchant. On a sudden, an immense blaze surrounded the house, and a cry of fire was heard in all directions. Annabella, throwing a few vestments about her form, descended to the door. On descending to the door, she opened it, and perceived that the fire was only a deception; and she was returning, when she was seized by several men, and hurried into a close chariot, which drove away with the rapidity of lightning. The whole party stopped at the market place. One pillar of it was hollow; and, being pressed by one of the party, disclosed a door, through which they all descended into an apartment below. It was hung with red satin, well lighted up, and elegantly furnished. A large sofa was drawn to a table, on which were placed fruits, conserves, wines, and refreshments of various kinds. One of her conductors, whose manners were in the highest degree polished, with a graceful wave of his hand, invited her to partake of them. Annabella, that she might be able the better to encounter any trials that might await her, sat down with easy elegance, and partook of the refreshment. In order to put her guide as much as possible off his guard, she conversed with a cheerfulness foreign to her heart, and praised the elegance of the apartment, and the flavour and beauty of the fruits. Her companion politely begging pardon for the necessity he was under of leaving her by herself, withdrew with a graceful bow through the pillar. Annabella now thought she might effect her escape; she therefore went towards the pillar, when two gigantic blacks, with drawn swords, opposed her passage, and compelled her to resume her seat. Annabella sat down discontentedly, and was lost in a thousand reflections. "I am destined," thought she, "to be the wife of some ferocious barbarian; but, if he can procure such fruits and wine as this, the life may not be altogether unpleasant. But then, my dear unknown! aye but his heart is occupied with a dead love. Can he furnish such an apartment as this? But then to live both day and night under ground, and by candlelight, to see no one of my own sex to whom I might impart my splendour, and be gratified by her envy; this, too, is horrible. O angelic form! O lover pointed out by the sainted Ethelinda! I will never desert thee! the frame of Annabella shall only be united to the form of I know not whom," added she with a stifled groan.

She had scarcely uttered these words, when a noise of springs was heard, the door of the pillar opened, and a form, covered with blood, tottered in; and, falling on the sofa by Annabella, fainted away!

CHAPTER X.

THE Armenian lifted up his hand to strike the ill-fated lover of Annabella; but, as to think and to act is the same thing with highly fertile minds, Thomas instantly seized his pillow, held it before him, and the dagger of the insatiable enemy entered the middle of it. Thomas immediately sprung from the couch; and, struggling with the Armenian, got possession of the dagger. He followed the Armenian, who retreated towards the wall, and covered him with wounds. The Armenian when he reached the wall touched a spring, and a door opened. He entered, smiling contemptuously at Thomas; and, banging the door in the face of Thomas, laid the son of Jeremiah senseless on the floor. On his recovery, he laid up the dagger in a drawer, and determined to overcome his repugnance to speaking to his family. The dagger would furnish ample proof of the truth of every thing he asserted. "What daggers and Armenians?" screamed Jeremiah, when he heard it, "what lictors and pictors* is the fool talking of? live low, boy, mind your business; give up these idle fancies, or you'll never be your own man again. Odd ferret it," said Jeremiah, "when I was a young man your grandfather would have laced my jacket for half an hour before he would have suffered me to talk such a pack of hocus pocus." "But the dagger," said Thomas, opening the drawer where he had deposited it; when, to his infinite astonishment, he saw a case knife; which, during the night, had been placed there by an emissary of the Armenian. "Oh, oh!" screamed the old man with a bitter sneer, "a nightmare!"—"A night-mare!" re-echoed the family. At last, half ashamed, and half indignant, Thomas pushed them all out of the room, locked the door, and threw himself into a large armed chair by the side of the fire.

CHAPTER XI.

ANNABELLA, whose tender mind was ever on the alert for fresh opportunities of exertions, balanced whether she should cut off the head of her Armenian enemy in his swoon; for by this she should perhaps free herself without exposing him to the least degree of alarm or inconvenience. But when she reflected on the blacks at the door, the vengeance of the unknown persecutors to whose machinations she was exposed, it occurred to her to conciliate his favour by paying attention to him in his present state. She was much at a loss what to do for linen, for she wore neither cap nor pockets; and to make a diminution in her chemise would expose her to the anger of her mamma, in case she should ever return home. The Armenian's turban met her eye in this perplexity, and tearing it into bandages, she bound them round his wounds, while he continued still in a swoon. It happened, that while she was engaged in this humane office, her garments touched the secret spring, which communicated with two folding doors. They instantly flew open, and discovered to the wondering eyes of Miss Annabella, an immensely long cavern, to the end of which the rays that issued from her lamp were unable to extend. Fear pervaded

the breast of Annabella; but fear, if it rises in the breast of
a heroine, only rises to be subdued, and is more to alarm
the reader than herself.* Immortal originals of the present
day! how well have you taught the female mind to despise
all terrors, real and imaginary! as if dungeons, subterraneous halls, caverns and passages, accompanied with ghosts,
daggers, snores, and groans, were of no more consequence
than a walk in the dark from the dining room to the drawing room.* In your heroines you reverse the story of the old
painter, instead of one copying many, many have copied
one; but, as there can be only one thing which is perfectly
right, you do well to follow it. Forgive your imitator these
observations! and, heaven bless me! forgive me Annabella!
for I have left thee, all this while, standing in a current of
cold air. Heaven grant there be no need of bran tea; for,
if thy tender epiglottis should croak like an American bull
frog, I know not, as things go in the cavern, how or where
to make it. But I forget, there is no precedent for a cold; a
fever is something; but the croaking of a cold, with all the
rags and bags, and paraphernalia of a sore throat, is neither
interesting nor heroical, so now for the cavern.

It was not without some emotion that she perceived
five hundred niches in the wall, and in every niche a sleeping robber, with an immensely long dagger lying by him.
Heroines, it must be known, have an instinctive and heredi-
tary skill in physiognomy; Annabella determined to exercise it, and accordingly, examined attentively the ferocious
countenance of each of them. There were two hundred and
fifty on each side; and, to her great amazement, she found
that one half were men of ferocious, and deeply brutalized
minds; while the others were men of fine feelings, delicate
conceptions, and of highly moral, though misguided under-
standings. It disturbed her to behold men, whose talents
and virtues would have done honour to any rank of society,
whose graceful demeanour, and highly polished conversa-

tion, would have been an ornament to the drawing room of a princess, buried in obscurity. It grieved her to behold them, undistinguishable by common observers, from the bloody and determined barbarians who lay opposite to them. The heart of Annabella was convulsed with contending passions, the orbs of vision were suffused, and dropping a pearly tear on the cheek of each of those good and feeling men, she bestowed a burning kiss on the lips of the last; but so soft, so tender, and so fragrant, that he dreamt a rose had touched his lips in the garden of an eastern monarch; so polished and so elegant was his fancy.

Ye powers, who teach us what people think and say to themselves, assist me in these and similar descriptions!

A thousand different projects entered the mind of Annabella; whether to kill them all with their own daggers, without minding the immense quantity of feeling, of susceptibility, of polished and elegant sentiment which would be lost to the world, by the destruction of these good and feeling men. However, it was not absolutely certain that every movement of the dagger would produce the intended effect; and if, at the end of one, or two, or three hundred, or four hundred men, an escaping groan should awaken their companions, the rest not knowing her motives, nor the pity which pervaded her mind for the two hundred and fifty good and feeling men, might possibly be offended at her conduct, and to testify their resentment would at least prevent her escape. It then occurred to her to awaken all the good and feeling men, by strings connected to all their toes, so that the affair might be done all at once by a sudden jerk, then to incite them to kill, as gently as they could, their brutalized companions.—They could then escape together, and seek her unknown and mysterious friend, who, she was convinced, would reward them handsomely; and, by a little coaxing, might be persuaded to forget his dead love, and marry her. The thought was ecstasy; and, in imagination,

her burning lips again under the lamp, pressed the cheek
of Thomas! This project, though sufficiently feasible, she
was inclined to reject, for fear some exclamation, escaping
from her suddenly awakened friends, might rouse the bad
part of the community, that a combat might ensue, from
which it would be difficult for her to glide away unhurt.
This though induced her to try a more calm, easy, and sat-
isfactory project.

Annabella possessed various accomplishments to which
we have alluded, or if not, the reader ought to have concluded in his own mind, that she possessed them; in fact,
the word heroine includes every possible perfection both of
body and mind. It would not be worthwhile for the historian
to write, the printer to print, and the publisher to publish
accounts of ordinary persons, when nature has produced, as
in the instance of Lady Caroline, women who have all the
virtues of heroines, without any of their faults.* I say, then,
that among the various accomplishments of Annabella,
she possessed a thorough knowledge of music. To rise to
perfection she confined herself to one instrument. It was
an instrument, from the form and construction of which,
being extremely simple, was probably of high antiquity;
though we cannot say positively whether it was invented
by Jubal, or made use of by Amphion, in the construction
of the walls of Thebes;* it gives ample scope for the expression, susceptibility, feeling, in fact, every power of the performer's mind. Its name betrays its eastern origin, it being
called by the northern nations the Jews' harp. Annabella
had acquired such skill in this instrument, that, if she played
in the fields, the cows and horses crowded around her; if in
her father's mansion, her venerable mother's canary bird
strained its little throat, (vain thought!) to equal and sur-
pass it. Such was the effect of its dulcet tones, that the most
obdurate heart could seldom avoid granting requests which
were made after its sounds. Rigid was the eye which refused

to suffuse its orb at its mournful sounds, and dull the heart which would not dance responsive to the cheering notes of the harp of Annabella.

Annabella, fully convinced of her powers in music, as well as in physiognomy, determined to give utterance to the sweetest, most mysterious, and most dulcet sounds, that ever issued from the instrument of a sublunary being. Strains such as these have been heard, or have been reported to have been heard, from Pan, or the mountain nymphs, by the sides of groves and mossy fountains. She prepared to infuse these sounds into the sleeping ears of the humane and polished robbers; and, as they awoke, to endeavour to gain their good will by sweet winkings of her eyes, graceful bendings of her head, and such wreathed smiles, as the care required by the instrument would admit of. In order to conceal the music, the light, and her graceful demeanour from the eyes of the brutal and bloody minds of the other robbers, the sweet girl held one of her woolen vestments before the light and the harp, so that the sight of her form, the light of her lamp, and the sweet and mystic sounds of her harp were all hidden from them. Every thing being disposed in this manner, the sweet girl began her progress. Her form was graceful as a mist that glides on the Ganges, and mysterious as those forms, which are seen at midnight, flitting over the pyramids, or gliding among the gloomy catacombs. After a few preluding strains, she had the pleasure of seeing a sweet and languishing smile on the countenances of the good and feeling robbers. In the lapse of a few moments, she perceived their brows relax, their mouths gracefully smile, and their whole countenances gradually assume the heavenly purity of infant cherubs. If it would not have consumed too much time, she would have dealt out kisses with a liberal lip on the lips of those innocent, and to her ever-amiable beings. "Pure and innocent beings," whispered she, overcome by her feelings, "never shall I forget your benevolence, if the harsh fates shall place me among burning sands, frigid snows, and ditches full of crocodiles, the thought of your pure and elegant minds shall cheer my aching and solitary heart. As each of them awaked, she gave him a smile so full of benignity and tenderness, that the robber felt his mind suffused with sympathy and happiness. She gracefully whispered her name to all of them, told them she was miserable, and begged their assistance. Having done this, she majestically retired into the adjoining cavern, leaving her elegantly polished friends in an agony of delight. When she was gone, they with one accord started from their couches, and withdrawing into a corner of the room, they joined in a tremendous oath, that they would ever protect the graceful form they had seen, if human, and requiring protection, from the bloody and ceaseless machinations of their bloody and hateful colleagues.

CHAPTER XII.

As soon as Annabella had returned to the cavern in which she had left the Armenian, and had closed the secret doors, she went towards the sofa, where she had placed him. In a short time he uttered several very deep sighs; and, at last, gently moved his head, and, with the assistance of Annabella, sat up on the sofa. When he learned, by inquiry, the assistance Annabella had given him, he thanked her in the politest terms, though he appeared greatly incensed at the loss of his turban, and rising up he shewed her a closet stuffed with lint, rags, and many surgical preparations. "This," cried he with involuntary anger, "will prevent the necessity of tearing up whole clothes; but," cried he with parsimonious brutality, "had you no linen of your own that you could have used?" "No," cried she, "not so much as a pocket handkerchief." At the suddenness of this reply the

Armenian frowned; and Annabella, recollecting her intention of conciliating him, was silent. The Armenian gracefully opened a drawer, and presented her with a newly washed pocket handkerchief, scented in lavender. "If," said he with an insidious smile, "the sweetest of all possible Annabellas would condescend to be my co-mate, she should want neither handkerchiefs, neckkerchiefs, headkerchiefs, nor any kind of kerchief which she could possibly desire." Annabella was silent, for she wished neither to encourage nor absolutely to reject his suit. If the unknown should be backward, thought she, one might meet with a worse match than an Armenian merchant; at all events it is best to be civil. At length she told him that her highly agonizing feelings, and her finely-wrought sensibility, had made her think but little of the marriage state; "but," added she with a sweet smile, "we shall see." The Armenian seemed satisfied, and gracefully entered into polite conversation with her, and displayed such stores of learning and observation, such copious knowledge of the customs and manners of every country under heaven, that Annabella forgot locality, and for some minutes imagined herself in the drawing room of a duke. At the first pause in the conversation, she asked him if he liked music, and understanding that he did, she uncovered her harp, and drew forth such sweet, heart-thrilling meandering sounds, sounds as of another world, that the heart of the Armenian gave itself up to inexpressible rapture, and he fell back on the sofa, in an agony of rapture. Annabella painted in sounds the distress of a virgin, immured underground, after having been torn from the embrace of her parents. Then she ventured on the plastic instrument to hint at the happiness of her return; and, to end her finely variegated strain, she concluded with a highly-wrought description of the delights of a honey-moon; with a view, in the background, of dancing cherubs and of infant angels. The reader may easily imagine, from this slight sketch, the amazing

perfection to which Annabella had attained on this instrument, and how little able a mind of ordinary texture would
be to resist its effects.

The Armenian was so far overcome that he could
scarcely live, and could only return his thanks in a convulsed bow. At last a gloom overspread his countenance,
and he looked about in a kind of confusion, like one who
has forgotten something on his return from the market
town. He drew a small whistle from his pocket, and sounding it, a young man, of graceful and majestic demeanour,
issued from a secret door. The Armenian beckoned to him,
and giving him a small piece of parchment, with a black
seal annexed to it, the youth, bowing gracefully to him and
Annabella, instantly retired.

CHAPTER XIII.

THE reader will shudder when he is informed that the paper
was actually an order for the murder of Thomas. It was
couched in the following words: "To all whom this may
concern; destroy Thomas, the son of Jeremiah, by any
means in your power, and as soon as possible. Dated from
the secret chamber, midnight!" The emissary who was thus
employed, was a man of a moral turn, and was unwilling
to imbrue his hands in blood. For this reason he had procured a new rope, well waxed, and, introducing himself
into the chamber of the son of Jeremiah, by means of a
spring which the Armenian lent him, he suddenly clapped
the noose about his neck, and hauling him from his bed,
before he was well awake, he left the form of Thomas suspended on a hook! By chance Jeremiah had been disturbed
in the night by the dreadful noise of cats on the tiles near
his windows; and, after this, by an eternal noise of water
dropping through the chimney on a saucepan which he had

accidentally left on the hearth; and towards morning, as he was sinking into a sweet sleep, he was still farther annoyed by an exacerbated dissertation of Jacintha, on the domestic economy of the last month. Not without a certain degree of fury, Jeremiah dressed himself and left the room. It occurred to him that he would go to the room of Thomas, and see if he had anything more to say about lictors, pictors, and Armenians. It was with the utmost grief and astonishment that this tender parent beheld his son suspended by a waxed rope from a hook! His first impulse was to cut the rope with his knife, but perceiving that it was a very good and serviceable rope, he began deliberately to untie it, that, at all events, he might be so far reimbursed for the vexation of the night and morning. After having released his son, and chafed his neck, Thomas uttered a groan, and looking up, saw his father. "Now, father," cried he, "will you believe in the machinations of the Armenian?"—"I will believe in the machinations of the devil," returned the father, with a bitter sneer, as he left the apartment with the rope. Thomas, incensed at the brutal parsimony and unbelief of Jeremiah, took his hat, and sauntered out to a favourite ruin in the neighbourhood. The stillness of the scene, and its sublimity, were peculiarly calculated to call forth in a mind imbued as his was, melancholy impressions of the past. The wrecks of former grandeur, with which he was surrounded, led him to reflect on the instability of every thing earthly. "Alas!" cried he, stamping with his foot at every word, "where is Babylon? where is Persepolis? where is Rome?" "Pieces," added he in agony, "have been torn from the pyramids, the frame of Thomas itself will be one day added to the general wreck!" "Nay," added he, "had nearly fallen a victim to the efforts of an Armenian and a waxed rope!" His feelings overcame him, and stamping more violently on the ground, he suddenly sunk into profound darkness. The reason of his sudden descent was as follows: in his agitation he trod

on the brass head of a spring connected with a trap door!
In a moment afterwards he was dazzled with the light of a
lamp, and saw the form of a ruffian, habited in black vestments, and masked! In one hand he held a pistol, and in the
other a dagger. The desperado immediately rushed up to
the son of Jeremiah, and fired the pistol, and aimed a blow
with the dagger at Thomas. The pistol bullet knocked off
his hat, and by good fortune the dagger entangled itself in
the neckcloth of Thomas. Thomas struggled with the ruffian, and threw him down, and was about to bore a hole to
his heart with a gimlet which he had in his pocket, when
four men approached with lamps. Thomas started up, and
pursued by the five men, ran through a long dark passage.
By good fortune he hit his head against a spring, which, let-
ting him through the wall, closed instantly on his pursuers.
Disappointed of their prey, the ruffians departed, with tremendous ejaculations; and the frame of Thomas, unable to
support the succession of horrors, sunk down in a swoon!

CHAPTER XIV.

WHEN every thing in the cavern was in perfect rest, Annabella having touched the spring, advanced, with a lamp in
her hand, to the long cavern, where she found both her
friends and enemies in a state of the most profound repose.
She bestowed many looks of cordiality, not unaccompanied
with tears and kisses, on the sleeping forms of her friends,
while she ever and anon regarded the bloody party opposite
with looks of horror and detestation.

Before she commenced her mysterious nightly music,
she advanced to the end of the cavern, that she might search
a mysterious antique coffer, which she had observed on her
last visit.* On opening it she saw the vestments of robbers,
intermixed with those immensely long daggers which we

mentioned in a former chapter. At the bottom she observed the form of a man, either dead, or in a state of insensibility. She lifted it out of the coffer, and, to her grief and alarm, she beheld the countenance of her unknown love; this being, in fact, the place where the spring had let in the form of Thomas, who had not yet recovered from his swoon! A dagger was sticking in his neckcloth; but, on taking off that garment, she saw no wound inflicted by it, but, to her great agitation, she saw a black mark, as if made by a cord, round the neck of Thomas! She felt disgraced; for she at first imagined that the supreme executioner of the law had laid his hands on the throat of Thomas, on account of some action of an immoral tendency. The thought was agonizing, but she instantly rejected it. "No," cried she, "the pure soul of my love would not have admitted a thought, much less a word, which could imply a dereliction from moral rectitude. Perhaps, poor man! he has hanged himself for Annabella."

Her next thought was what to do with the body, and at last she concluded, that whether he was alive or dead, the best plan would be to disguise him in the vestments of a robber, and to place him in a spare niche among her friends, with a dagger by his side. Accordingly she arrayed the form of Thomas in the habiliments of a robber, and deposited it in a spare niche among the two hundred and fifty good and feeling men, that, in case of recovery, he might be in good hands, and his moral character be in no danger; so tender was she of the reputation of her lover, even when she had reason to believe that he was numbered among the dead! Having performed her celestial music, in the same manner as before, she gracefully withdrew.

Thomas not long after awaked from his swoon, and seeing the vestments of a robber, by the light of a lamp near him, he concluded that he was either in a dream, or that it was some other person, and immediately sought relief in sleep. In about half an hour he waked, and giving himself a tremendous pinch on the cheek, was too fatally convinced of his being in a waking state. "What am I," screamed he in a voice of horror to himself, "and where am I! alive or among the dead, in my senses or out of them, above or underground! Am I Thomas, or a robber! if I am Thomas, why am I here! if I am a robber, why am I without nefarious sentiments?"—Thomas was ignorant that there were lying near him two hundred and fifty robbers of the purest, of the most virtuous sentiments, men who, without the least change in their sentiments, might, in strict justice, have arrayed themselves in sacerdotal garments. If the son of Jeremiah could have examined their countenances with a lamp, he would have found the thing written up in characters sufficiently plain. As it was, he was all doubt, amazement, and dismay. If he had not retained some confused idea of the pain of dying, he would, with his dagger, have made an aperture for the exit of his confused spirit. He was lost in confusion.

————————"He reasoned high,
But found no end in wand'ring mazes lost."
MILTON.*

CHAPTER XV.

THE next day, at dinner, the two hundred and fifty virtuous and humane men, being seated on one side of the table, and the brutalized and bloody ruffians on the other, Annabella was placed at the top of the table, and the Armenian seated himself at the bottom. Annabella beheld the form of Thomas among her friends; but still confused, still agitated, still doubtful whether he were Thomas or a robber, or both, or neither. His lovely face, from the late determination of blood to the head, had assumed a purple hue, such as nature, with her gentlest hand, lays on the mulberry, sweet child of Autumn, and more rarely on the stem of the celery. His nose and his lips, from the doubts which had pervaded his mind, were of the deepest white: on the whole, it was impossible for the imagination to picture a more complete image of interesting loveliness. The black mark, which was seen at intervals round his neck, gave an air of intense horror to his countenance, which suited well with the scene around him. The lips of Annabella could have dwelt with rapture on every part of that black line, if, as her mind augured, it had not been made by the executioner. Otherwise, forbid it, heaven, that a Tit should kiss any part of the form of one just fresh from the hands of Jack Ketch.* But if that sable mark, as her imagination painted to her, had been caused by some virtuous exertion, if the form of Thomas had been suspended to save a father, a mother, a brother, or a friend, then she could dwell for ever on that delicious spot. "But," added she, in a scream of horror to herself, "if he has been hanged in disguise, for any friend who has committed immoral acts, then is the lover recommended by the dead Ethelinda disgraced, and Annabella undone for ever! In no country do they make a practice of suspending men, except of nefarious characters; and, if he has been hanged, how has he escaped?" "Perhaps, after all," added she with a kind of shudder, "it may be the ghost of Thomas: dreadful thought!" To relieve herself from this distress, she shed a shower of mental tears; for she thought it bad policy to weep outwardly, lest it might displease the Armenian. Sweet girl! she was unwilling to displease even an enemy. She composed her countenance in such a manner as to make sundry significant signs to her friends, while to her enemies it preserved a composed civility. The heart of Thomas was alarmed, for he thought she was in love with one half of the community, and jealous of the other half. To ease his agitation, which she saw through the purple tinge of his countenance, and having no appetite, she uncovered her harp. Her task was difficult; especially since the art of curing epilepsies and rheumatisms, by music, has been lost.* It was to humanize the minds of the ferocious robbers, by musical thoughts, drawn from religion and morality, to give a history of her life, feelings, and wishes to her virtuous friends, to ease the heart of Thomas, and to inform him of her name and family; and, at the same time, not to discourage the hopes of the Armenian. The attempt was arduous, but to her skill not impracticable, and completely successful. She saw bad thought after bad thought, nefarious project after nefarious project, vanish from the minds of the bad robbers; but, ah! what depths of wickedness remained! how many touches of her harp would it require to purify and defecate* their contaminated bosoms! Before this can take place, thought she, the form of Thomas, if still living, may have descended to the tomb, and the dust of Annabella, mingled with the winds of heaven, may be blown into the eyes of some sensitive damsel, or love-encumbered hero! The thought was horror! Annabella uttered a deep but inaudible groan. At this moment the eyes of the Armenian and Thomas met for the first time. They were both perturbed, alarmed, and dismayed; and, after a vacant stare of some moments, they both fell down in a state of insensibility.

CHAPTER XVI.

EVERYBODY, of both parties, the bad and the good, rushed forwards to the assistance of Thomas and the Armenian. Annabella immediately arrested their progress; and, by the notes of her harp, directed the bad robbers to put the Armenian to bed; and the good, to convey the form of Thomas to the mansion of his father. Annabella had no immediate desire of escaping; in the cavern she had nothing to do, and

was eating and drinking of the best. She had not quite concluded on relinquishing the Armenian; and, at all events,
was determined to have no further intercourse with Thomas
till his character and countenance were a little cleared up.
It happened, that one of the friends of Annabella, in com-
pliance with the nefarious demands of the Armenian, had
often entered the chamber of Thomas. This man, with
three more, conveyed the form of the son of Jeremiah to
the house of his father, and having laid him on a bed, they
gracefully retired.

When Thomas recovered from his swoon, he saw Jeremiah and was beginning to say, "Now, father, what do
you think of the machinations of the Armenian?" when that
tender parent burst into tears, and asked him what was the
meaning of that strange garment? "O, Thomas! Thomas!"
sobbed he, "you will be the death of your poor mother and
me; do dress yourself in your own clothes, and come down
and help me." What it was, in which Jeremiah wished the
assistance of his son, that we may soften the melancholy
truth as much as possible to the reader, we will leave him to
guess for a whole chapter. In the mean time we will return
to Annabella.

CHAPTER XVII.

THAT sweet girl, having ordered the Armenian to be laid
quietly on his couch, and having harmonized his mind by
a few divine touches of her harp, was going to leave him,
when, suddenly, he started up, and screamed "What have I
seen? the ghost of Thomas! the injured shade of him I murdered!" "Murdered!" shrieked Annabella, starting back accidentally on the button of a spring which immediately let
her through the wall. The place in which she found herself
was the ancient burying place of the robbers! To her great

surprize, she observed that almost all of the tombstones
were marked with the names Robert Tit, Abraham Tit, and
Nicholas Tit. She felt immediately assured that they were
the ancestors of the humane and elegant robbers; if so,
delightful thought, these polished beings were her cousins,
and ought to be tenderly embraced in the arms of their relation. She determined to examine the tombs more minutely.
The words on the tomb of Nicholas Tit were, "Here lie the
remains of Nicholas Tit, Lord"—the remaining part of the
stone was broken off. "Heaven and earth, sea and land!"
cried Annabella, in an ecstasy of joy, "am I then descended
from a Lord? I know it, I feel it! I always thought myself
better than all the heroines of the town." A doubt occurred
to her mind, that the words might possibly have run thus:
"Here lie the remains of Nicholas Tit, Lord have mercy on
his soul." She recollected, too, that the noblemen who came
to the town were called, Lord A—, Lord B—, and Lord C—;
not A— Lord, B— Lord, or C— Lord. This doubt rather
distressed her, but the sublimity of her conceptions, and
the loftiness of her ideas, convinced her that she must be
of noble extraction. "Can these hands," cried she, "whiter
than the virgin lily; these cheeks, which blush sweeter than
the rose of Tifflis;* these eyes, which outshine the diamonds
of Golconda,* have been ultimately descended from a ple-
bian Tit?" It immediately occurred to her, that she had seen,
in the beginning of a book, Francis Bacon, Lord Verulam;
the reasoning was convincing, nothing remained but the
name of the title.* She examined the ground attentively,
and at last found the word "Muckfield," which seemed to
fit on tolerably to the word "Lord." It was clear then that
her great ancestor was "Nicholas Tit, Lord Muckfield." She
revolved in her mind other great personages who might be
allied to her; when the name of Emperor Titus* occurred. It
was plain that he must be allied to her, Titus being nothing
more than Tit, with a Latin termination.

Having formed these conclusions she walked majesti-

cally into the other cavern, and sat down with conscious
dignity by the side of the Armenian's couch.

CHAPTER XVIII.

I⊤ is not without a considerable degree of hesitation, and a
painful delay of three days, that we have, at length, assumed
sufficient courage to approach the reader with the informa-
tion of the occupation of Jeremiah. Modern ears have got so
devilish delicate, that they have almost separated the ideas
of dignity from utility. The employments of patriarchs and
heroes are esteemed mean and degrading. We shall first
raise the reader's fancy by a few lines of Homer; and then, to
avoid wounding the ears of the reader, we shall describe the
occupation of the father of Thomas, by a circumlocution.

> "With that the chief the tender victims slew,
> And in the dust their bleeding bodies threw:
> The vital spirit issued at the wound,
> And left the members quiv'ring on the ground."*

In fact, the occupation of Jeremiah was to deprive of life
the forms of certain beings, and then to deal them out in a
mercantile capacity. The frame of a sheep was then hanging
in an apartment below; and, dreadful to relate! the father
of Thomas desired that hero to strip off its outer integument, and to divide it into parts, for a mercantile specula-
tion. Thomas obeyed; though, of course, reluctantly, and
having finished the disgusting office, retired with a majestic
and graceful step to his own apartment. Thomas, being at
leisure, instantly made a sign for the four-and-twenty lictors
to appear; who, gradually insinuating themselves through
the keyhole, appeared in a humble attitude before Thomas.
Their looks were pallid and perturbed; and, in tremulous
tones, they informed him, that a deep plot was formed

against him, in which their four-and-twenty successors, though humane and virtuous men, were, by the machinations of the Armenian, obliged to assist.

Having said this, without staying for any further questions of Thomas, they spread their light wings, and immediately flitted through the window. As when a flock of pigeons have alighted in the plains of Ariconium, fast by the wandering silver-streaming Vaga,* if perchance a boy had thrown a stone into the midst of them, they rise with speed to the clouds, so flew the lictors through the window of Thomas. Thomas endeavoured to catch the foot of the last lictor, but without success; he fell, and in falling caught the leg of a table, the table fell against the broom, the broom against a looking glass, and the looking glass breaking, destroyed some old china, with which Jacintha had decorated the mantelpiece of Thomas. This united din irritated Jeremiah and Jacintha, and they ascended the stairs with immense broomsticks in their hands. "It was a lictor," cried Thomas, as they opened the door; "I'll lick you," said Jeremiah; so saying, he and Jacintha assailed the form of Thomas; as, when in ancient and barbarous times, before threshing machines were invented, two sturdy labourers assailed a sheaf of wheat. They grow warm with their work, and the grains of corn fly about the floor; so Jeremiah and Jacintha grew warm, and the dust flew from the coat of Thomas. Thomas dared not resist the sacred forms of his parents, but suffered patiently, till at last he fell down in a state of insensibility. Jeremiah and Jacintha were frightened, thinking they had killed Thomas; they accordingly laid him on the bed, and gracefully retired. They shed many tears, when they reflected on the expense of the funeral solemnity, and the loss of the occasional labour of Thomas. "I am afraid he is gone with the lictors and pictors," groaned Jeremiah. "I hope not," said Jacintha; "I'll go up and see." Instantly she warmed some aqua vitæ,* and had the satisfaction to see

Thomas sitting up in his bed, and reading a small piece of parchment, with a black seal annexed to it. It was left in his room by the lictors, who intended to shew it to Thomas, but had forgotten it. These were the words: "To the four-and-twenty lictors; destroy Thomas, the son of Jeremiah, by all means in your power, and as soon as possible. Your lives shall answer for your failure." Jacintha trembled; and, shewing the writing to Jeremiah, they determined, by all means in their power, to preserve Thomas from the machinations of the Armenian!

CHAPTER XIX.

ANNABELLA was sitting by the side of the Armenian's couch, and contemplating him with looks of fixed disdain and indignation. "And is it you, you vile underground rogue," cried Annabella, "who pretend to marry the descendant of Nicholas Tit, Lord Muckfield? Sooner would I be united to my unknown lover, if he had not only been hanged but gibbeted." So saying, and being seized by a sudden fury, she seized the Armenian by the beard, and shaking it desperately, to her great surprize, it came off, together with the outer part of all his face. Annabella looked to see whether she had done the Armenian an irreparable injury; when, to her astonishment, she beheld the smooth, soft, and august countenance of the mayor of the town. The fact was, the pretended Armenian had concealed his face, and his nefarious projects, under a mask! Nefarious rogue! he had an old wife who was wheeled about in a chair, and of whom he was heartily tired. It was his project to unite himself with the form of Annabella, even while his wife was living. It must, however, be confessed, that he knew nothing of Annabella's descent from Lord Muckfield, so the relations of that illustrious nobleman will have no cause to impute any studied insult to the mayor.

The fact was, that this nefarious magistrate, at least till he had heard the music of her harp, was by no means aware of her being a heroine; and, to his vulgar and undistinguishing eyes, she appeared no greater than the daughter of Tit, the greengrocer! The pretended Armenian, enraged at the double discovery of his face and his projects, sat down instantly to a writing table, where, with the utmost rage painted on his countenance, he filled a small parchment with writing, and affixing the mysterious black seal of the secret cavern, he rung a small bell, and three men rushed forwards, habited in black vestments, and masked! After having read the parchment, they seized Annabella, and, in perfect silence, dragged through several dark passages the form of the heroine.

The three men now produced a key, and opened a door in a large column through which she saw a dusky and spiral flight of stairs, leading far underground! Into this opening Annabella was ordered to descend by her companions, who paid no regard to her assurances of her being perpetually troubled with rheumatism in damp places. Annabella was forced down into a small room, the door closed upon her, and she heard it bolted on the outside.

Sinking on the damp floor, she was lying in a torpid state of agony and despair, when something cold and clammy crawled over her hand, which was stretched on the floor of the dungeon. Shrieking with affright, she hastily arose, and supported her fragile form against the damp wall, till reminded of her situation by a desperate twinge of rheumatism! She thought she had been too rash in rejecting the attentions of that cold and clammy being. Perhaps, thought she, (consoling thought!) it was some friendly being; and we shall see that the event justified her thought. Through a wish to avoid the feeling of intense solitude, which she now entertained, the sweet girl was determined to explore the dungeon in every direction, that she might discover the

companion which the harsh fates had given her. She felt
almost everywhere, but she felt in vain. Our heroine gave
over the search, and began to feel a sensation which even
the noblest minds feel when united to this body. Such is the
harshness of fate! In fact she longed for some nutriment,
and, like our princely Henry, had divers strong recollections of that vulgar compound small beer.* "What," cried
she, in a voice of agony, "if this pretended Armenian should
have resolved to separate my ghost from this mortal coil!"
"But," added she, in a voice of vengeance, "if so, my soul
shall stalk forth as thy avenging tormentor:

"Then Tit shall come in a black sulph'ry flame,
When death has once dissolv'd her mortal frame;
Shall smile to see the traitor vainly weep,
Her angry ghost, arising from the deep,
Shall haunt thee waking, and disturb thy sleep;
At least my shade thy punishment shall know,
And fame shall spread the pleasing news below."
DRYDEN'S VIRG.*

Annabella was not long in this state of perplexity; she
almost instantly heard the heavy tread of a man in the passage, who entered the dungeon. After having left some
bread and meat, a small pitcher of wine, and a larger of
water, and a lamp, with a bottle of oil, he left the apartment. Our heroine earnestly begged for a few yards of flan-
nel, in case of a rheumatic attack; but the man, frowning
horribly, denied her request. When he was gone, she examined the dungeon more minutely for her cold and clammy,
though probably warm-hearted, visitant. To her surprize,
she saw nothing but an immense toad in the corner. With
an instinctive horror for that animal, which misses generally think proper to have, Annabella at first shrunk back.
The whole contour of this animal, and the turn of his eye,
at once shewed him to be far superior to the common race

of toads. There was a mild benignity and intelligence in the sweetness of his smile, which shewed that he had enjoyed some intercourse with superior beings. While Annabella was hesitating whether to stay longer, or to return to her seat, the animal gently croaked out the word "Peter," to the great surprize of Annabella, and shortly after the word "Pholy." "Peter Pholy," whispered our heroine, in the gentlest manner possible. Peter seemed to listen with pleasure, and hopping forwards, seemed to meet her advances in the most amicable manner. From this time he was her plaything, her love, her Peter, her dear Pholy. Peter would without help climb up on her knee, and look into her face with the most endearing and innocent affection, for Peter was far from entertaining such nefarious projects as the pretended Armenian. Annabella, observing in him so many traces of intelligence and good will, determined to try what might be effected by the powers of her harp. Accordingly, when Peter was sitting on her knee, she uncovered that instrument, and by degrees elicited the whole of his story.

"He had been," he said, "in the former part of his life, an unfortunate toad. He was persecuted by evil-minded boys, and had no fixed home. About the middle of his life, he had so far attracted the patronage of a beneficent gentleman in Staffordshire, that he gave him a convenient tenement, under a loose stone in his greenhouse. He was happy, he said, easy in his own mind, and beloved by others. This state continued, till one day a millipedes, or rather a devil, in the form of a millipedes, enticed him from his home, from his dear and never-to-be-forgotten patron. The night was foggy, and he missed his way. As it often happens to men and brutes, when once in the wrong to wade farther into error, so Peter, the more he tried, the more he wandered from his dear greenhouse, and at last had fallen suddenly into his present habitation. He had lain for some hours in a state of insensibility, but had afterwards every reason to be satisfied with his condition; "for to be perfectly happy," he observed, "was the lot of few, or none. To enjoy a little, was better than to be bored in great possessions;" with more moral apothegms than I have leisure to repeat. "It is not," concluded he, "my intention to quit my present habitation, unless I hear some certain news of my beneficent patron. I have here food enough, I am never troubled with boys, and seldom with men; I am contented to live, for the present at least, in obscurity, far from the retreats of men;

> "The world forgetting, by the world forgot."
>
> POPE.*

CHAPTER XX.

"TIT!" screamed Jacintha, when Thomas had finished his adventures, which he was relating to her. Jeremiah sighed "O Tom!" "Tit!" screamed Jacintha again; "is it possible that the blood of the Baileys can mingle with a Tit! Jeremiah, my dear, what was it that you whispered to me last night, when I could not sleep for the wind, about the nobility of your family?" "I will tell you," said Jeremiah, assuming an air of majesty, "you must know that my great grandfather, Mr. Alexander Bailey, was a Jerseyman, of course of the old Norman blood; Jersey being, as you have read, or if not, for you don't care much about books, Jersey being, as I tell you, a portion or parcel of the old Duchy of Normandy. My grandfather used to tell me, that his father often said that his great grandfather told his father that an ancestor of ours, in the time of Robert Duke of Normandy, held an office in the stable or kitchen of that prince. Now you know, Jacintha, that those who serve sovereigns are noble. He being noble, we, as being lineally descended from him, are also noble, though the title is forgotten. Now I have never had fortune enough to bear a title; not that I am ashamed of being a

butcher; the devil claw him, I say, who is ashamed of his
trade, whatever it be. Now if you, Thomas, could persuade
your lictors or pictors to point out a bag of money, win the
title and wear it; but as for Tit's whining daughter, if you
speak to her again, I should make no bones of splitting your
head with a cleaver." So saying, he walked majestically out
of the room.

The spirit of Thomas was fired, and he was determined
to avoid all possible intercourse with Annabella, till the dignity of her birth should be made out as unequivocally as his
own.

The reader will have seen how well we have made out
that affair, and how well the several parts of our plot go
hand in hand together, and how, in imitation of our illustrious contemporaries, (may their heads lie softly on their
pillows) we have passed from Annabella to Thomas, and
from Thomas to Annabella. Our chief care has been to keep
probability in view. It is not enough for a thing to be possible, it must also be probable. It is not enough, to put off the
reader with the old proverb, that le vrai n'est pas toujours le
vrai-semblable.* A good writer, among which number we
hope the reader will not scruple to place us, should explain
any unusual occurrence.

These remarks have been called forth by the incident
of Peter Pholy, in the last chapter. We are afraid that many
an ignorant reader will pronounce it a fiction from beginning to end. The fact is, that the speech of Peter was not
actually made as it stands there. "Then the whole is a lie,"
exclaims the ignorant reader. Patience! We have only made
use of a privilege common to us with Livy, Herodotus,* and
other historians, of putting into the mouth of our characters words suited to his situation, without minutely examining whether he actually spoke them or not. The thoughts
were chiefly inferred by Annabella from sundry croakings,
winkings, and contortions of the said Peter. As to his real

existence, if the reader is not convinced by making proper inquiries in Staffordshire and Nottinghamshire, we will give him leave to cut off our head, and stew it down in soup for the poor, for which we shall leave our direction with the bookseller.

Having condescended to say thus much of possibilities and probabilities, we expect the reader not to quarrel with any little incidents which may be laid before him. The best and safest way, my good friend, is to give yourself up into the author's hands; "be pleased you know not why, and care not wherefore."*

CHAPTER XXI.

"WHAT an excellent blue sugar bason have you got there," said Jacintha, to Penelope Dodler; "bless me! what a pretty pattern! I declare I'll have just such another! How much did it cost? Where did you buy it?" "At the new glass-house, Madam, set up three days ago; I went there with Jedediah; there would be no end to my buying things if Jedediah, miserly wretch! had not kept twitching my gown all the while. "What opportunity for Thomas," said Jacintha to Jeremiah, "to improve himself by seeing glass made; you know what pretty taste he has; who knows how many pretty things he may buy!" "Who knows indeed!" sighed Jeremiah. "Besides," said Penelope, the man who shewed me all the things together, said he wished of all things to have Mrs. Jacintha Bailey's opinion on some new patterns, her taste was so universally known." "Oh, Madam," said Jacintha, "you surely flatter me about taste; experience I have a little in matters of taste, but as to taste itself, oh Madam!" "Come, come," said Jeremiah sternly, "if you wish to know anything about the glass-house, pray send Thomas, for if this oily-tongued fellow, with his nonsense about taste, should meet with you, Jacintha, he would make you pay for his compliments, by making you an infinity of blue, green, red, and cut glass; here, Thomas, put on your new coat, and take this half guinea: if you should meet with any bauble your mother may like, buy it." Thomas immediately obeyed the commands of his dear father, not at all suspecting that the whole affair of the glass-house was a machination of the Armenian, to insure his certain destruction! Several of the robbers had built this glass-house for the sole purpose of enticing the son of Jeremiah into it, that they might attack him by himself. They were bent on his death, for an immense slaughter of the members of the secret tribunal had taken place, on account of the repeated escapes of Thomas. These members rejoiced exceedingly when a centinel on the top of the building informed them of the approach of the descendant of Alexander. When he came to the gate, and rung the bell, a civil personage, smiling and bowing extremely low, preceded Thomas into the interior. The eyes of Thomas were agreeably entertained by the immense variety of green, blue, short and long, cut and uncut glass. He was never tired of questioning his civil guide, and was feeling his half guinea with a kind of half resolution of making some desperate purchase, when he was not a little surprized at receiving a wound in the head, by the hand of his obliging companion! The descendant of Alexander turned round to receive some apology, when his eyes beheld the forms of the ministers of the Armenian, and he felt himself completely in their power. Despair sunk deep into the mind of the lover of Annabella Tit, but, with a graceful wave of his head, he told them to do their worst. Immediately on a sign given by their Captain, whose name was Steballino, a ruffian, from the neighbourhood of Turin, they immediately fell on our hero with axes, hammers, knives, and pokers, for the space of half an hour, covering him with wounds, and completely spoiling his new coat.

Mr. Thomas Bailey smiled on them contemptuously, and his mind wandering from the busy scene around him, dwelt on former mysterious scenes; the picture of Ethelinda arose in his mind, with her magic music, and the cavern scenery. "Perhaps," thought he, "I may never see her more." The thought was agonizing to him, he could no longer endure it, when suddenly his attention was arrested by a violent and tumultuous ringing at the outer gate. The banditti appeared alarmed, and the countenance of their chief exhibited every appearance of mysterious perturbation. It was first red, then pale, then red again, then turned to a bluish cast, and at last subsided into a mixture of all three! The ringing at the gate became more and more tumultuous and exacerbated, when a horrid crash proclaimed that the outer door had yielded to the efforts of the intruders. The Captain looked mysteriously at the banditti, and they descended, one by one, through the trap door, which opened by a spring, after having thrown Mr. Thomas Bailey into a furnace of melted glass.

CHAPTER XXII.

ANNABELLA having, by the assistance of Peter, discovered the hole by which he had descended into the cavern, and having given an affectionate kiss to that faithful friend, whose philosophic turn of mind she could not sufficiently admire, ascended once more into the open air, and with slow and majestic steps sought her father's mansion. She found that parent not only vexed at her long absence, but also exceedingly angry, for he imagined that she had taken to some bad course of life. She wished to clear up all his doubts, but, to her great astonishment, Abraham would not believe a single word that she told him about the Armenian, the equal division of the good and bad robbers, the dun-

geon, and Peter Pholy. She determined no longer to consult
that obdurate parent, who so sternly refused to listen to the
voice of reason. It should be her first endeavour to find out
the form of her lover: if he could clear up his character, she
would do the same office to his visage, by some May-dew,
and other washes, of which she inherited an ample supply.
There lived in the house of Abraham an ancient nurse, who
had been servant to Mrs. Tit, the departed mother of Annabella, to whom she had communicated many secrets. When
fate released Mrs. Tit from this mortal coil, old Ergathea
transferred all her affections to Annabella. Ergathea was
the daily resource of Annabella, against the brutality of her
father. In the apartment of Ergathea hours dissolved into
moments, in the recital of stories full of high and frenzied
sentiment, and acute sensibility. It was there that Annabella learned to feel herself a heroine, and to know that
she was far superior to the common offspring of common
women. Ergathea, for she was a woman of sense, refine-
ment, and reading, of course gave her belief to the account
of Annabella.

Ergathea told her there was not the smallest doubt of
the honour of Thomas; he might have been hanged by accident or mistake, or treachery, but from his physiognomy, as
related by Annabella, she was convinced that his character
was inviolate. With this conviction, she was willing to bear
a letter to the descendant of Alexander, appointing a meeting near the ruined tower. Ergathea immediately went,
under some pretence, to the mansion of Jeremiah, and
inquired for Thomas. The venerable Jacintha, with tears in
her eyes, told her that Thomas had not been heard of since
the morning when he went to see a curious manufacture of
glass. Jacintha said, that she herself had inquired there, but
found, that after having staid a short time, he had left the
building. Jacintha had given sixpence to a boy to seek him
in every part of the town, but in vain. She was apprehen-

sive that he had fallen into the hands of an Armenian lictor, who she knew would never be satisfied while Thomas was alive. Often and often had he attacked that dear form by himself, and others. Once by means of waxed rope.— "Good heavens!" cried Ergathea. "He made," said Jacintha, "such a black mark round his neck that he will carry it to his grave!" Ergathea clasped her hands together, and stood in an ecstasy of joy: "Then he is innocent," cried she at length, "and Annabella will be happy."

"Annabella what?" angrily asked Jacintha. "Tit!" answered Ergathea. "Tit!" screamed Jacintha, "Tit me no Tits!" So saying, with the violence of a West Indian thunderbolt, she pushed Ergathea, the tender confidante of Annabella, from the house, and rudely slammed the door like a whirlwind in her face!

CHAPTER XXIII.

IT was fortunate for Mr. Thomas Bailey that the ruffians being wholly intent on the prosecution of their infernal attempt, had let the heat of the fire very much relax, otherwise the lover of Annabella Tit must have suffered very much, or have lost his life in this adventure. As it was, he has often confessed to me that he never felt so completely uncomfortable in the whole course of his life. Though his blood was stanched, his coat was spoiled, and he was left in that condition in which the ingenious housekeeper of a nobleman, or gentleman of fortune, leaves a currant or barberry, after an immersion in melted sugar. In fact, he was completely cased in glass; and, if a light allusion may be admitted in so serious a subject, he resembled one of those preparations which the anatomist hands round to his admiring class.

The persons who so fortunately preserved Thomas from death were a German count and his attendants. This

German, from his frequent potations, had rendered a temper naturally irritable completely furious and ungovernable. In consequence of this, he demolished every thing that stood in his way, men, women, castles, glass bottles, chairs, tables, and windows. He had just arrived in town, and on inquiring after its curiosities, was informed that it contained nothing curious but a new manufacture of glass, of all colours, sorts, sizes, lengths, and depths. "Drive me there immediately," cried he in a furious tone to his coachman. In a short time, he was at the gate of the manufactory. When he found that nobody attended to the bell he grew furious, and ordering his servants to borrow hammers and iron instruments from a neighbouring artist, immediately forced a passage into the interior. The count stalked majestically forward, and finding nobody there, in a fit of rage demolished all the glass within his reach, and departed.

When Thomas, who was by this time very eager to quit the manufactory, heard that his deliverers were gone, he got out as well as he could, and soon found that the motion of his form in walking had made something like joints, so that he could walk as easily and expeditiously as that redoubted champion, who even yet has the boldness to appear at coronations.*

It happened at a neighbouring forge, about a year before this unprincipled attack on our hero, that two of the men, Francis and Oswald, having quarrelled, Oswald fell unfortunately under a descending sledge hammer, which by some accident instantly killed him. His companions stood around his pallid remains, expressing their sorrow by their countenances and uplifted hands. They were in extreme doubt how to proceed, whether they should call in any body, or if any body, whether the constable, the coroner, or the mayor. While they were still hesitating, a low sepulchral voice was heard to proceed from the distorted remains of their departed comrade: "Bury me in the middle of the

room, and say no more about it." This injunction of the
deceased they religiously attended to; a few pots of water
cleared the shop and hammer of all marks of the late catas-
trophe, and the few who inquired after the poor Oswald,
were persuaded that he was gone in quest of fresh employ-
ment. But conscience, that active power which never lies
dormant, except it be very well paid for doing so, began to
entwine itself imperceptibly into the hearts of these men.
She embodied the defunct spirit, and persuaded them that
it regularly walked every night. The belief of this, accompanied by latent whispers, and confused communings, pervaded the manufactory. Things were in this state, when
our hero was proceeding slowly towards the shop, in order
to procure the aid of Francis, with whom he had become
acquainted at an association at an auberge in the suburbs of
the town.

Our hero was perhaps the first lobster who so earnestly
desired to have his shell broken, and to be taken out of it.
He appeared at the door, and three times uttered, in a voice
like that of the departed, the name, "Francis, Francis, Francis!" The mechanics hearing the sounds, were dismayed at
its hollow cathedral tone, and perceiving what appeared to
their eyes a dishuman appearance, unnerving fear recalled
to their minds the image of their lost comrade. They fled in
all directions, and Mr. Thomas Bailey, with a majestic step,
and as gracefully as he could, entered the deserted shop. To
a mind like his thinking and acting were simultaneous operations. His mind devised the project, and his body obeyed the
impulse. In an instant he was under a descending hammer.
The first blow cracked his glassy integument, the second
broke it in every direction, and the third disengaged the
form of Mr. Thomas Bailey, who sprang lightly on the floor,
by no means desirous of encountering another blow.

As when a caddow worm, which a fisherman has skill-
fully disengaged from its scaly coat, and is just ready to put

on the hook, by some convulsion of his enemy's finger slips into the brook, well pleased to seek a new coat, so Mr. Thomas Bailey rejoiced to have escaped from his integument; and, gliding gracefully from the shop, by a postern gate, entered his father's mansion.

> "So from the ruins of expiring Troy,
> Aeneas snatch'd his father and his boy;
> Through the rough seas, and rougher lands, they fly,
> And rest at length in fruitful Italy."*

CHAPTER XXIV.

THE arrival of Thomas was not long concealed from the ears of Ergathea, who knew that the happiness of Annabella depended on a union with the frame of Thomas. Now the innocence of that hero was fully proved, reason, religion, susceptibility, and every human inducement made this connexion a matter of paramount necessity. For this purpose she disguised herself as a Jew, and pretended to a great skill in medicine, having heard that Thomas was very much indisposed, and was troubled with a kind of fever. In fact that hero, as the reader may well imagine, was by no means well. He was troubled with considerable burning, which he tried to ease by the application of cold keys, oils, foxes' tails, jellies, and pieces of marble, without the least effect. It was then with great joy that Jacintha heard of the arrival of the Jewish physician, whom she immediately introduced to her son. Ergathea tenderly approached the bed, and taking Thomas by the hand, bade the son of Jeremiah take comfort. "Annabella," said she, "is yours, body and soul; witness, thou silent moon, before whose pale orb she has so often poured out her burning suspirations; witness, ye winds of midnight, who have been enlarged by her sighs; ye cataracts, whose foaming waves have been increased and salted by the tears of the descendant of Nicholas—" "Of Nicholas!" said Thomas, "you must mean Abraham." "No," said Ergathea, rising with majesty, and gracefully waving her hand; "I mean the descendant of Nicholas Tit, Lord Muckfield. Did'st thou suppose, Thomas, that the smell of vegetables, and a few dealings in a mercantile capacity, can obliterate a noble birth? If Abraham Tit, merchant, before the birth of Annabella, has soiled his hands in commerce, can that heroine help his being a green— I cannot repeat the odious word!"

"I, too, am noble!" cried the descendant of Alexander; "the blood of the Baileys has flowed to us from a Norman origin; some of it has flourished in a Norman court.

"What we are now—I too have my delicacies; I too cannot mention the odious word. What have Nimrod, Alexander, Cæsar, with an infinity of others, been before us? The noble soul stalks out from obscurity, and wanders like a comet through infinite space; surveys the ring of Saturn, penetrates beyond the flaming walls of the world, and darts into the profound abyss of eternity."

"Eternity! thou pleasing dreadful thought!"*

"The soul of Thomas, disdaining the co-mates that the harsh fates have given him, looks up to nobles, secretaries of state, and premiers; rolls from the concert to the play, from the play to the concert, with the countesses and duchesses, and revels with the kings, the potentates, the emperors, and Kesars of the world! Air and ocean! comets and double stars! blood of the Baileys! interminable honour!" So saying, Thomas fell back exhausted, in a state of insensibility. The venerable Ergathea beat the palm of his hands, tweaked his nose, and used sundry other methods till the form of the descendant of Alexander revived. Ergathea then settled upon a meeting at midnight, near the ruined tower;

and, bowing low, left the descendant of the follower of the
Duke of Normandy to his meditations.

CHAPTER XXV.

THOMAS and Annabella having settled the time of their
meeting near the ruined tower, by the means of their confidante, expected that scene with phrenzied feelings and high
susceptibility. On the morning which preceded that auspi-
cious night, Ergathea, aware what would be the effect of
that meeting, borrowed eighteen pence of Annabella, in a
mysterious manner. Annabella asked with some surprize
what it was for? Ergathea only answered with a mystic
shake of her head, and with a benignant waving of her
hand—"You shall see." This benignant old matron accordingly purchased some spirit of salt, some lavender drops,
and procured some cold water in a bottle. With nippers she
cut off from some of Abraham's sugar, conveniently formed
knobs for receiving the lavender drops for Annabella. To
this she added some aqua vitæ for Thomas, and several req-
uisites for susceptible and fainting lovers. Beneficent being!
may'st thou never want eighteen pence to purchase a drop
of soothing liquor, while thy ghost remains involved in this
mortal coil!

As an historian I am approaching a tremendous crisis;
help me, fair reader, and may heaven bless you with a
Thomas, if indeed nature has formed a second model of
perfection, help me, I say, with your recollections, your fancies, your susceptibilities; in short, imagine yourself to be
Annabella, and your lover Thomas, and all will be well.

The clock had struck the hour of midnight, when Annabella ascended the hill leading to the tower, leaning on the
arm of Ergathea: her heart beat high, and her step was trembling and unassured. The bird alive in the hand of its taker

was but a faint emblem of Annabella. Sweet lily, blown by
the winds of tender sighs, and watered by the tear of affection, may the mildest genius of love guide and protect thy
footsteps!

But who is this coming from the opposite side of the hill,
bedewing the tender flower with his tears, mingling his sighs
with the winds of heaven, and occasionally tottering to the
earth with the violence of his love? It is, it must be, Thomas.
They approach! they are nearer to each other, they totter to
the earth, they rise with difficulty, they embrace, they faint!
Ergathea had prepared a knob of sugar moistened with
lavender drops, she inserts it into the mouth of Annabella.
She applies the neck of the bottle to the mouth of Thomas.
Heavenly powers! they revive! They press on mutually to
their trembling bosoms. But what is this? they faint again!
for heaven's sake, Ergathea, ply thy restoratives. After each
fresh fainting, Ergathea restored them in the same manner,
but, at last, seeing a light at a distant auberge, she descended
the hill with rapidity, leaving the forms of the two lovers
extended in a state of insensibility.

Ergathea speedily returned, bringing with her a bowl
filled with a compound called punch, and a pipe with some
tobacco, and a small lantern. When she had recovered
the lovers, she addressed them in these words: "Progeny
of Alexander, and thou, descendant of the great Nicholas,
let us go to the tower, and there pass the hours of night in
sweet and solemn converse, not unmixed with the joys of
Bacchus." The lovers obeyed, and tottered to the tower.

"That delicious mark!" sighed Annabella, "shall I kiss
it?" "You shall," said Thomas, opening his collar. Annabella
fixed her burning lips on the spot, and Thomas was in an
agony of ecstasy. In this manner they entered the tower.
Annabella made the hill re-echo with her harp, and Thomas
tenderly presented her with a silver nutmeg grater, and a
printed pocket handkerchief.

The morning star now danced over the mountains,

and the first rays of the sun warned them to return to their respective homes.

CHAPTER XXVI.

THE lovers had not observed a tremendous form, which mingled with the midnight breeze, and surrounded the tower where they were sitting. It was the form of Jeremiah Bailey, who had often peeped into the tower, and was highly irritated at their nocturnal conviviality. He departed in a rage, bestowing, mentally, many names which were not soothing to the female ear, on the venerable Ergathea. "As for that cursed Tit," said he, "I'll contrive some way of sending her out of the country."

When Thomas got home he went to bed, tired and exhausted, after having first inserted his form in an oil-case bag, filled with cool emollient oils, to take the fire out of his burning frame. Jacintha drew the string round his neck, and tenderly wishing him repose, gracefully withdrew. She had not left the room five minutes, when Thomas heard four men enter the room, who taking him up in the bag, retired in a graceful manner through a concealed opening. Thomas was alarmed, for he well knew the author of this machination. The reader will be surprized when he hears the contriver of this plot. Not to keep him in suspense, it was no other than the wily Armenian. Thomas heard the steps of his enemies directed towards the sea, and hearing them mention it, was terribly alarmed lest they should end his days in its salt waves. In fact, they entered a small sailing boat, bearing with them the bag containing the body of the descendant of Alexander. When they arrived at the mid-sea, between England and France, after a mysterious consultation together, they threw the bag and Thomas overboard, and immediately sailed away!

It is remarkable that, about this time, many stories were

in circulation about mermen and mermaids.* These were
no other than Thomas, who was seen floating by ignorant
mariners, the bag appearing to their eyes like the tail of a
fish. We just mention this observation, in order to set the
minds of philosophers at rest on that subject, it not being
probable that there are such beings. It happened that a
report of this kind prevailed at this time through France,
insomuch that Buonaparte, who either is, or pretends to be,
remarkably curious in natural history, issued an order to
all Admirals, and captains of ships, all prefects, governors,
to all princes, judges, treasurers, counsellors, and sheriffs,
and all police officers whatever, to bring him a mermaid
with all convenient speed. Great was the bustle through-
out the whole coast of France. If two men were talking
together, one always heard the word "Mermaid;" if one
man asked another how he was, he answered, "have you
seen the mermaid?" In short, the anxiety was so great, that
a sea captain, one morning, found his body completely covered with scales, with certain finny protuberances about his
fingers; and a poor woman, in Holland, was delivered of a
dead fish! At last, the captain of a three-decker one after-
noon, being terribly intoxicated, ventured out upwards of
a quarter of a mile from the shore. He would have gone
farther, but an English frigate just then hove in sight. On
his return he espied something floating on the water. The
head had the appearance of something human, and the tail
looked fishy. "Out with the long-boat," cried he, "and bring
it up."—While part of the men were thus employed, he
ordered others to bring a large turtle-tub on deck, and fill it
with water. In the mean time the long-boat returned, bringing the pretended mermaid, which the reader will be surprized to hear was Thomas! He was instantly immersed in
the turtle-tub, excepting his head, and the ship returned to
port. The sailors amused themselves with the likeness that
his face bore to a human countenance, and laughed heartily
at his hissing gabble, which they affirmed could never be

a real language. The people of the seaport crowded about the mermaid, and admired it exceedingly, and several philosophers petitioned the Emperor for leave to dissect it when it should die, to which his Majesty returned the most gracious answer, which delighted the whole nation. In the mean time the turtle-tub was hoisted into a low cart, and forwarded to Buonaparte, who, by good fortune, happened to be on the coast.

CHAPTER XXVII.

WE are anxious lest some readers, who do not reflect, might suppose that we have a little violated probability, to account for the floating of Thomas. And here we do positively and honestly assert, that by a bag we mean a bag in its literal sense, and in no metaphysical or metaphorical sense whatever, simply a sack or pouch to put anything in. This we say in deference to some noble and polished persons whom we wish to class among our readers, and whose approbation both in this, and all other things, we should be too happy to attain. We shall conclude our digression by observing that, in its metaphorical sense, it is more likely to sink a man than to float him.*

Buonaparte was sitting in a large room, surrounded by his marshals, when the turtle-tub was introduced. Delighted at the thought of having his curiosity gratified, he approached the tub, when to the surprize of everybody, he cried out, "bless my heart! this is not a mermaid, but Thomas!" "Thomas!" screamed everybody; "yes," said he, "Thomas, the son of Jeremiah, the descendant of Alexander, the progeny of a nobleman at the court of Robert Duke of Normandy, the lover of the dead Ethelinda, and the living Annabella."

Some readers may wonder how he knew all this. The fact is, that he knows the concerns of every individual in

Europe, better than the individual himself does, and besides, the Armenian was his emissary. That nefarious character had agreed to smuggle an army of a hundred thousand men into the midst of England, and destroy the independence of the nation in a moment. The Armenian, in a confidential letter, had informed Buonaparte of the adventure of the waxed rope, and that wily Corsican knew him by the black mark, and uttered the foregoing words to give his attendants a high opinion of his sagacity. Thomas gracefully bowed assent to what the Emperor said, and observed, in courtly terms, that as he was not a fish, there was no necessity for his spending the remainder of his existence in a turtle-tub.

The Emperor ordered vestments suitable to the birth of Thomas to be brought to him, and whispering mysteriously with his marshals, after politely apologizing to Thomas, he left the room. Thomas immediately dressed himself, and seeing an immensely long and sharp sword lying near him, he secreted it in his vestments, not being willing to leave himself entirely without arms in an enemy's country. While the descendant of Alexander was musing in his own mind on the strangeness of his condition, Buonaparte entered majestically, and smiling, for his smiles are the sweetest things in nature, charmed the whole of his court. He was followed by an infinity of personages splendidly dressed, and among them figures who had on "the likeness of a kingly crown," and at the end of this pageant, "an apparition of a child crowned—"

> "That rises like the issue of a king,
> "And wears upon his baby brow the round,
> "And top of sovereignty."
>
>   MACBETH.*

Thomas was much inclined to laugh at this, thinking it intended for a joke; but, on seeing the demure looks of the court, and piquing himself on being one of the best bred

men in Europe, he instantly checked himself. To his great
astonishment there followed two men, bearing a crown on
a crimson cushion, and after them four, bearing an empty
chair of state. They set it down by Thomas, and the court
maintaining a profound silence, the Emperor addressed
him in the following terms: "Thomas, son of Jeremiah,
descendant of Alexander, I create thee sovereign Duke of
Normandy, on the simple condition of secretly conveying
fifty thousand men into the heart of England." The whole
assembly concluding that the consent of Thomas would
follow of course, rushed forwards to crown Thomas. But
that hero waving his sword, and crying with a loud and
stern voice, "avaunt, ungracious hypocrites! and thou,
perfidious upstart!" The whole assembly fled to the other
side of the room, and Buonaparte instantly touching a concealed spring, an immense portcullis fell between them and
Thomas!

CHAPTER XXVIII.

THE rumour of the loss of Thomas could not long be concealed from the inquisitive ears of Ergathea, who immediately informed Annabella of that circumstance so fatal
to her peace. Everyone commiserated the misfortune of
Jacintha, who had not only lost her son, but an oil-case bag,
worth five shillings and threepence. "What a son! what a
bag!" cried Annabella. "Double calamity! ill-fated parent! O,
my last found, best-beloved Thomas!—what grave conceals
that head, and that lovely variegated neck, from the eyes
of Annabella? Some waxed rope, the seeds of which were
sown in thunder, and reaped at the execution of a mur-
derer, has made a tighter compression on that throat on
whose black mark the graces were wont to sit. Where were
ye, O ye nymphs of groves, fountains, and ruined towers, at

the fall of Thomas? ye certainly were not in the bed-room
of Thomas."

> "Ay me! I fondly dream
> Had ye been there, for what could that have done?
> What could the muse herself that Orpheus bore,
> The muse herself for her enchanting son,
> Whom universal nature did lament,
> His gory visage down the stream was sent,
> Down the swift Hebrus to the Lesbian shore."
>
>   MILTON.*

"Oh! Ergathea, help me to ascend to my chamber, my
grief shall not be opened to the eyes of a green— Oh! oh!
And, Ergathea, I may again faint! bring up, I pray you, a
little of that delicious compound, whose taste will bring
to my mind the form of Thomas!" So saying, she slowly
ascended the stairs, at every step she gave a groan, and at
every landing place she fainted.

Oh! Annabella, hadst thou known the sufferings of thy
Thomas, thou must have died outright. Heaven and earth!
To have thy Thomas mistaken for a mermaid, and immersed
in a turtle-tub! It was to her great comfort that she heard the
form of Ergathea climbing the stairs with her restorative.
They sat hand in hand on the side of the bed, adding their
warm tears to the warm liquor. The last drop was drained,
and Annabella, through a violence of her grief, fell senseless
to the floor: Ergathea immediately started up to assist her,
but something having caught her foot, she tottered, and fell
by her side, and having joined in her grief, that venerable
matron lay extended in a like insensibility. Delicious pair
of friends! may the graces strew over you their softest rose
leaves! Ergathea lay in that state until it was dark, and the
cold zephyr, breathing through a broken pane, somewhat
revived her. She rose, though chilly and exhausted, and
undressing Annabella, deposited her grief-stricken frame in

a bed. Ergathea herself followed, and Morpheus shed over them his choicest poppies!

Night after night did Annabella lament her Thomas; night after night did she fly to her restorative, but in vain! The purple face of that hero, and his mottled neck, haunted her imagination, and would not let her rest. She wandered at midnight near the ruined tower, regardless of the beating storm which, unmindful of the fair face exposed to it, was raging inextinguishably.

Annabella shrieked out "Thomas, Thomas!" and the melancholy echoes returned the words "Thomas, Thomas!" It was a maddening reflection to her that these words were not heard by the being whose name they designated. One night, as she was walking by moonlight near the tower, she was surprized by the sight of a man above the middle size, who issued from a broken part of the wall. She imagined that the end of her life was fast approaching. It might be one of those bloody banditti who often rob, and murder the innocent contemplators of moonlight scenery. In this state of mind she was determined to disappoint the ruffian as much as possible; and, for this purpose, she threw behind a bush the silver nutmeg grater, and the printed pocket-handkerchief, representing the victories of Nelson, the dear remembrance of the lost Thomas! In the mean time, the mysterious stranger advanced, and discovered not the countenance of a robber, but the no less dreaded visage of Mr. Jeremiah Bailey. Instead of the anger and dreadful denunciations of vengeance which she expected, his countenance was meek and insidious. "Dear bereft innocent!" said he, grasping her hand affectionately, "I am ashamed of my cruelty: by the lucent lunar orb that hangs over us, I will never more afflict thee."

Annabella was softened, the heart of the Tits was always tender: bright beaming drops suffused the orb of vision, and she felt for her printed handkerchief. It was mysteriously

absent; at last, after some confused recollection, she sighed
out, "it is behind the bush." "What?" interrogated Jeremiah.
"My handkerchief," uttered she, with a graceful whisper.
The parent of Thomas, with a majestic step, passed behind
the bush. "It is found," said Jeremiah. "Pray then," said she,
with a persuasive smile, "dear parent of my Thomas, if
affection for me has warmed your heart, pray look for my
silver nutmeg grater too."

> "And now perpend, ye gentle lordlings all,
> That hence to France we may convey you safe,
> And bring you back, charming the narrow seas
> To give you gentle pass."
>
> SHAKESPEARE.*

CHAPTER XXIX.

"WILY Corsican!" cried Thomas, with a voice of thunder;
"if your country had not shewn me that minute portion of
hospitality in the turtle-tub, I would have dashed through
your gratings, and immolated thee and all thy satellites to
the manes of half Europe. As it is, if ever thy foot venture
on another land, that moment the brand of Thomas shall
drink the blood of Buonaparte."

This anecdote furnishes a real key to the caution with
which Buonaparte has abstained from appearing personally
in Spain. It is neither his indolence nor his uxoriousness, but
his fear of Thomas. Those who are ignorant of secret history are obliged to invent reasons for the conduct of great
men, which we, who are admitted behind the scene, have
ample reason to laugh at. The whole conduct of the war in
the peninsula, with all its brilliant detail of events, has been
ascribed to the present ministry, without the least mention
being made of Thomas. Those who are sceptical about the
existence of Thomas must give them the whole undivided

praise; but they should first, by a careful perusal of all the registers in the kingdom, prove his nonentity. At all events the warmest thanks of the nation are due somewhere. But to return to our kings and Kesars. Buonaparte having exerted his whole power to keep up his resolution, found at last that his courage was not equal to a full view of the horrific and superhuman Thomas. His face changed to an ashy paleness, his knees trembled, and he fell insensible into the arms of his attendants. Thomas has often told me that he saw none of the marshals who did not appear as capable as the Emperor of sovereign command. "Nay," added he, "if fortune had so willed it, Buonaparte might have been Thomas, and Thomas Buonaparte."

During his swoon, Thomas seeing that he had nothing more to do in France, stalked majestically to the shore. There he saw a gun-boat, fastened to a chain; he immediately leaped in, spread the sail, and steered for the English coast. To his great astonishment more than twenty boats sailed from neighbouring parts of the coast. These belonged to that corps of physicians which we mentioned in a former chapter, who having some doubts about the use of the pancreas, were determined to solve them by the dissection of a living mermaid. The boats gained upon Thomas, and the men at length entered his vessel, when Thomas leaped forward into the water, and swam deliberately towards the English shore. The boats having missed their object returned to the shore. Thomas swam on, and luckily found a hen-coop, which had accidentally dropped overboard from an English frigate. He seated himself upon it, and having found some tobacco, a pipe, and some means of striking a light, he immediately lit his pipe, and delivered himself up to luxurious reflections on Annabella. In the mean time a vessel, of the most curious form and construction that ever was made, appeared in sight; the form was that of a club, the sails were in the shape of a club, the

mast was a club, in fact the whole affair was a floating club.
It appears that some thirty or forty dukes, marquisses, and
earls had clubbed together to furnish this vessel, in which
they might enjoy each others' society without interrup-
tion, and might float after fine weather to every portion of
the globe. Their idea was singular, but their conversation
was so sprightly, so elegant, so thoroughly club, that Mr.
S— W—, himself, could he have entered the vessel, would
have been delighted.* Noblest and best of men! into whatever part of the globe the harsh fates shall throw the author
of this immortal work, it will be his highest consolation to
have seen and conversed with thee.

The crew of the floating club had long been contemplating the unusual spectacle which presented itself to
them; from the smoke which arose, they conjectured that
it was the effect of a sub-marine volcano. When they came
nearer, a common seaman would have pronounced it to
be Davy Jones* himself; and, in fact, it required more than
ordinary science to determine that he was not an evil spirit
condemned to that weary waste, or the wandering Jew.*
One of them hailed him, and inquired where he came from,
where he was bound to, what was his business, and who
he was. "I come from France, I am bound to England, my
business is to think of the dead Ethelinda, and the living
Annabella, and I am the Duke of Normandy." Immediately a silken rope ladder was let down from a gallery to
the sound of the sweetest music, and hollow parts of the
vessel being struck with clubs, gave so good a base, that
Thomas, being a man of the most refined taste, could not
stand under the ecstasy, but fell repeatedly from the ladder
into the sea, from which he was with difficulty recovered.
The supposed Duke of Normandy was ushered into the
state cabin, and desired to repose himself on a splendid sofa.
Thomas, gracefully inclining his head, addressed the splendid assembly in these words: "Gentlemen," said he, "when I

told you that I was the Duke of Normandy, it was more my intention to study conciseness of language than exact truth. I might have been Duke of Normandy. I have been in the presence of that wily usurper, who, arising from an island in the middle of the earth, has spread famine, horror, and desolation over half the globe. He offered me the dukedom on easy terms, which I rejected. A number of persons, with crowns on their heads, and little baby kings, tried to crown me by force, but I sternly resisted. Had not I thought it rudeness to have attacked him in his own chamber, that nefarious root of kings would have been cut off by the sword of Thomas. In other lands"—said he fiercely, and he said no more: the violence of his feelings reduced him to a state of insensibility, and the crew of the floating club tenderly inserted his form into a bed.

"And now to England do we shift our scene."[*]

CHAPTER XXX.

THE silver nutmeg grater being found, and the printed pocket handkerchief, which, though mashed in some mortar by the majestic foot of the father of Thomas, was not the less cherished as a pledge of the absent, and never to be thought of without agonizing recollection, Thomas. "Yes, by heaven," exclaimed she, squeezing the printed pocket handkerchief, with the mortar clinging to it, into her bosom; "yes, by the lucent lunar orb which I now look upon, wert thou filled with Jedediah Dodler's rotten turnips, which stink like the devil, when one pokes a stick into them, I would do the same to thee." When the tender and agonizing thought which perturbed her breast permitted her to be slightly conscious that she was still an agonizing inhabitant of the sublunary regions, she cast an hesitating look at her companion. Was it the effect of some treacherous thought lurking in his breast, or merely the hue arising from the spirituous and saccharine infusions by which, in moments of disappointment, he soothed his tortured breast? "Perish the thought!" said she, squeezing the tail of his coat with tender respect; "rather let all the Tits be sacrificed together on Salisbury Plain, and myself perish with an ague on the top of them, before the least grain of suspicion infect me, the least, the last, and the most afflicted of that illustrious family."

Annabella was introduced into the mansion of Jeremiah, who politely told her that he would send a messenger to Mr. Abraham Tit, to inform him that she would stay all night. "You are too good;" simpered Annabella. Jeremiah entertained her with music and the most splendid supper. At bedtime he lit a candle, and ringing for his servant, he gracefully put the candle into the hands of Annabella. Iphigenia conducted her to a superb chamber. But, though entertained in this sumptuous manner, our Annabella passed but a restless night; she half resolved to lie down in her clothes, as done by thousands of heroines before her, for she knew not what nefarious ideas might have glanced into the mind of the father of Thomas. "But," added she, "have I not heard or read, 'that vice may glance into the breast of a wise man, but it remains only in the bosom of fools.' Jeremiah is no fool. Besides, at all events, come what will the mind will retain its purity."

Those who have read "The Legends of a Nunnery," and "The Mysterious"—I forget what, will easily see the nice distinctions we allude to.* What a fine thing is learning! Happy age! when such a number of us take the trouble of instructing you: would to heaven the number of those who practice virtue did but half equal the number of those who teach it.—Annabella in the night was troubled by dreams and ephialtic attacks, which the vulgar call the night-mare. After the fourteenth ephialtic attack, which Miss Annabella

Tit experienced, as she was lying awake in a tremulous and confused state of mind, she heard the door gently open, and three women entered, bearing a small luminary. Their step was slow and cautious, and they whispered in a mysterious manner to each other.

CHAPTER XXXI.

THE crew of the floating club were highly delighted with Thomas; his conversation shewed a mind imbued with sentiments of honour and generosity.

> "A mind not to be subdued by time or chance."*

The crew with one consent offered to elect him a member. "Every thing," said the captain, "is made perfectly easy; we just lay down a thousand pounds a quarter."— "Oh!" sighed Thomas, in some confusion, "my father is"— "still living," added the captain, "that is your misfortune, and indeed ours, but it cannot be helped." Thomas begged the captain to set him on shore at the first convenient opportunity. In the mean time the club had been sailing about a fortnight, when the bold shores of Spain appeared in view. At this moment a French fleet appeared in sight, and an American coming up, told the crew of the floating club that the fleet was in search of Thomas. Now all nations respected the neutrality of this vessel, on condition of their not aiding any enemy.

The captain of the vessel, calling Thomas on deck, politely apologized for the necessity under which he lay, assured him that nobody would feel his loss more than himself, and then gracefully pushed him overboard. He then let down the hen-coop, with some tobacco and a pipe, fully satisfied that he had done no injury to Thomas by leaving

him as he found him; then, turning the rudder, he totally
forgot the existence of the son of Jeremiah.

CHAPTER XXXII.

WE left the reader in considerable anxiety about the fate of
Annabella, with three figures in the room, whose intentions
were probably hostile. We shall now proceed to relieve it.
The women drew her curtains, and by degrees removed her
bed furniture, and stripping the quilt from the form of Annabella, they retreated in the same slow and cautious manner
as they had entered. This proceeding, when the mysterious
events of the time began to be developed, was found to arise
from the parsimonious brutality of Jacintha, who cared not
whom or what she troubled, in order to increase the stock
of linen destined for lavatory operations.* Baneful effects
of distempered civilization, which disturbs the sleeping
and the quiet by untimely noises, injudicious clamour, and
moist perturbation! She arose about ten o'clock, in a feverish and highly unpleasant state of body, having recourse to
a cordial which she generally carried with her, to support
her mind in unusual circumstances. She then descended
with graceful and majestic steps to the eating room, where
Jeremiah was sitting majestically in a window, and gracefully reading the County Journal.

He rose to salute her with one of those soft smiles,
which he knew well how to impress on his countenance.
"Dear Annabella," said he, "delight of my lost Thomas, let
us amuse ourselves before breakfast in looking over the
house." Annabella bowed assent, and followed Jeremiah
through several rooms and passages. At length Jeremiah
stopped short in the middle of a long passage, where there
was not even the appearance of a door. "Here," said Jeremiah mysteriously, "I keep a tame magpie."—Annabella

began to grow alarmed. What could he possibly mean! Was he labouring under the effects of a disordered intellect, or was it merely a sudden delirium? "Heaven and earth! Sea and land!" sighed Annabella to herself; "what is possible to be done with a madman in a long narrow passage?" Mr. Jeremiah Bailey smiled mysteriously at her perturbation, and pressing the brass head of a nail, a secret door opened, and discovered a small room lighted by a skylight. The curiosity of Annabella was excited, and the friend of the lost Thomas entered. Immediately the door closed with a noise of thunder, and a confirmation of the truth flashed on her mind.

"Infernal monster!" screamed she in a voice of despair, "where is the magpie?" "The magpie is safe enough," sneered he. "Oh, ho, Madam, you thought I would marry my son to a Tit, did you! No, no." So saying, with a brutal laugh, he descended the stairs, and his heavy majestic step resounded through the house.

CHAPTER XXXIII.

THOMAS had acquired by experience so much skill in guiding his hen-coop, that he was perfectly easy. He lit his pipe, and smoked away, totally forgetful of every thing in the universe, excepting himself and Annabella. Nay, he was sometimes doubtful whether he himself was not the only thing really existing, and Annabella nothing more than an emanation of his own mind, tender indeed, and lovely, but unsubstantial as the dream of a lunatic. "This requires consideration," cried Thomas, swaying himself about in tremendous agitation; "if I am I, and there is nothing but I, then I can do nothing. The idea of Annabella will again rise in my mind." In this agitation he fell from the hen-coop, his tobacco floated away, and his pipe sunk to the bottom of the interminable ocean. "Ha!" said Thomas, "at all events

I have lost the idea of a hen-coop." He immediately swam forward, seized the hen-coop, and again seated himself on that vehicle. He was now totally at a loss for occupation. "I now," said he, "feel quite alone; my tobacco and pipe are as if they had never been." In this distress, he smote himself with his fist on every part of his body; at last his knuckles hit against some books, in the pocket of his vestments. To his great joy, he found a Spanish grammar, a dictionary, and a volume of Lopez de Vega.* Thomas applied himself with so much intenseness to his books, that in three hours he was a perfect master of the language, and could speak it with the fluency of a native. This anecdote places the character of Thomas in the highest rank of genius. It would be difficult to find a parallel. When he had given the last touch of per-fection to his efforts, he saw the whole French fleet just at his heels, "breasting the lofty surge.'"* He saw all their boats let down, and the crews advanced with swords and spears. Thomas pocketed the volumes, slipped suddenly from the hen-coop, swam ashore, climbed a mountain, and hid himself in a cave. The fleet, not being able to find Thomas, returned to port.

In a few minutes some peasants came into the mouth of the cave, to eat their usual breakfast of bread and grapes. One of them informed the others of the atrocious action of Buonaparte, in carrying away the King and Queen.* "Ha!" cried Thomas, with a voice of thunder, from the inside of the cave. The peasants trembled. The tremendous form of Thomas came forwards, and dashing his fist with violence against a rock, he broke it into a thousand pieces.

"Spaniards, can you bear this?" cried Thomas. "Not well;" answered they. "Swear then to revenge it." "We swear;" cried they. "Have you any influence over others?" "We can raise a village."—"So ho!" shouted Thomas; "have at you, Buonaparte."

Thomas searched the cave in every direction, and was

lucky enough to find a vast collection of swords and spears, which had been left there by the Moors. He told the peasants to bring him in every man able to bear arms: "With these," shouted Thomas, "we will easily exterminate the Corsican.—Shall we be slaves, Spaniards? Shall we butter the bread of slavery with the butter of oppression? Forbid it, Ethelinda; forbid it, Annabella; forbid it, all ye tutelary saints which flit about the mountains, and guard the independence of the Spanish name."

Thomas waved his sword, and shouted; and all the peasants joined in the shout. Their shouts rent the bosom of the earth, and enlarged the cavern so, that it would easily conceal ten thousand men. This gave great joy to them all. Thomas shouted out, "I will kill a hundred men a day, more or less; if every man will do half as much, we have nothing to fear." The multitude, which was now very great, shouted "A Thomas, a Thomas! may he live ten thousand years!" The son of Jeremiah, who had seen several corps of volunteers go through their exercise, had a perfect knowledge of the art of war. He squared them, and columned them, and triangled them, wheeled them and re-wheeled them, and made them cut and slash, and push, and curse and shout like ten thousand devils, with their tails cut off at the root.

Thomas, and a few of the most skilful, determined to pass from mountain to mountain, to find and make vast quantities of arms, while Garcia and Peublos, two experienced mountaineers, would follow up the hints of Thomas. Thomas advised them to send instantly to England for arms and assistance, and to conclude an alliance between that country, Spain, and the Indies. Thomas and his friends passed from village to village, and from mountain to mountain. The flame of opposition spread over the plain, and curled over the mountains.

"Now Ethelinda! Now Annabella! your Thomas is worthy of you. Now let fire mix with earth, ocean with air, and land with water; your Thomas shall ride securely on the billows, and frown at fate."

CHAPTER XXXIV.

HORRORS, and alarms of various kinds, imbued the head of the hapless Annabella. In all the involutions of her thoughts it was difficult to decide in what path to tread. Her person, that fragile form, it was evident, was very much curtailed in it locomotive faculty. "Yet the mind, Jeremiah, the mind, in spite of thy secret springs, and still more secret doors, shall wander ecstatic, from the ring of Saturn to the wall of China, from the whispering gallery in St. Paul's to the palace of the Emperor of the French, and back again, with superhuman velocity, to the agonizing remembrance of the lost, and to me valued above all things, Thomas."

In this manner she made a confinement which, to an ordinary mortal, would have been in the highest degree uncomfortable, in the highest degree ecstatic. But as all plans of life, particularly those which depended on bodily motion, were put a stop to, she determined to effect her escape as soon as possible. In order to effect this, she determined to lay aside the angry denunciations and contemptuous smiles, common on these occasions, and to put on the most persuasive smiles and winning address. "Who knows," cried she, "what may be done with Jeremiah? At all events, men are not like rocks, to be softened with vinegar."

When she had made this determination, she heard the secret spring touched, and the door slowly opened. Mr. Jeremiah Bailey, and his dog Phillis, advanced into the room. The sight of the dog called up a stratagem in her mind, which, as appearing in a slight degree improbable, I should of course be unwilling to relate, if it were not a known fact that heroines have very little trouble in deceiving those they deal with, by any expedient, however trifling, which they choose to adopt. Annabella then, for a particular purpose, determined to attach Phillis as much as possible to herself, and she was pleased to see that the animal visibly yielded to her blandishments. Jeremiah, softened by her manners, inquired "whether she found herself perfectly comfortable?" "Perfectly so," returned she, with a most enchanting smile, "but I should be more amused if I had some canvas, and a little brown and white lamb's wool, to employ myself in working." "You shall have some of Jacintha's immediately," said he. As soon as Jeremiah was gone, she revolved in her mind her stratagem. It was in effect this, to imitate as exactly as possible the skin of Phillis, to clothe herself in it, and by some device to go out with him instead of that animal.

In the mean time, she determined to imitate the whining tones, and fawning attitudes of the dog; and so much was the sweet girl taken up with this thought, that Jeremiah, on his return, found her on her hands and knees, and almost began to suspect that her senses were disordered. As soon as she perceived the father of Thomas, she pretended to have been seeking a pin, upon which Jeremiah presented her with two, which he had found in the suburbs of the town, and which his parsimonious nature had induced him to stick in his sleeve.

When the father of Thomas had departed, she sat down to her work with alacrity. Under her daedal hand the canvas gradually assumed the form and colour of a dog, and when it was completed, and she had put it on, and was viewing herself in the pocket glass, it required some force of mind to convince herself that an animal of the canine species was not actually before her. If this trick could impose on her acute and conscious mind, how much more would it deceive the comparatively dull and torpid intellect of Jeremiah! There was a little angular recess in the corner of the room; into this she determined to entice the dog, and tie her up, and having previously dressed herself, to issue forth in that character, and leave the room with the father of Thomas.

At his next visit, when Jeremiah had laid down some food, and was leaving the room, Annabella called Phillis, and tied her to a brass nail with a silk garter; then, with a trembling heart, she so well imitated the actions and prancings of a dog, that the most experienced gamekeeper would have been deceived. Jeremiah was deceived; and, tapping her on the head, they left the room together. At the end of the passage she separated from the father of Thomas, and throwing off her disguise, she glided gracefully down the stairs; and, by a postern gate, left the habitation of Jeremiah.

Fear added wings to the feet of Annabella, and she had almost gained a forest, planted by the attorney of the town, consisting of three dozen firs, two of larches, four beech trees, and an oak that would not grow; when, on looking behind her, she saw the tremendous form of Jeremiah advancing, with a sword in his hand, which he had found by accident in the path. When Annabella had escaped, in the ingenious manner above-mentioned, and had thrown off the disguise at the top of the stairs, it happened that the form of Jacintha glided by almost immediately after, in search of Jeremiah. She perceived the disguise, and enraged at the use which had been made of her lamb's wool, she flew towards the father of Thomas, and as soon as she appeared in his sight, Phillis began to bark violently in the secret apartment. A suspicion of the truth instantly flashed on his mind, and on examining the room, he found it empty. He rushed with great wrath out at the postern gate, and in a few seconds he perceived the form of Annabella floating in the evening breeze, at the entrance of the attorney's forest. Deadly passions filled his mind, and he determined, by one sanguinary deed, to avoid all possibility of contaminating his family by an alliance with the Tits.

While he was thus mentally employed he looked round and saw nothing but trees! It had happened, fortunately for Annabella, that she had by chance in her pocket a piece of canvas, on one side of which she had painted a larch tree, and on the other a pig-sty, being fond, in her hours of solitude, of elegant and refined amusement. In an instant it occurred to her fertilely copious mind to unfold the larch tree to the eyes of Jeremiah. "By Jupiter," screamed out the father of Thomas, "here must be some trick; I will search every tree in the forest before she escape." Thus determined, he proceeded to search every tree of the forest, not being willing to trust merely to his eyes. It now occurred to Annabella, that the parent of Thomas had a particular antipathy to pigs, and not to pigs merely, but to their habitations also, nay even to the name of pig. This antipathy arose from the following cause. One day, when he was a young man, he took a pig of one of his neighbours, by way of joke, as he often confessed afterwards, and was beginning to salt it, when unluckily the neighbour came in, and by some private marks knew the pig to be his property. Not being in the number of those who relish a joke, and persuading some persons, who had as little knowledge of humour as himself, to join the conspiracy, they actually incarcerated the father of Thomas. It is reported that he received some practical admonitions before he could be released, and in fact heard so much of pig, both in doors and out, that it quite tired him, insomuch that, even at this distance of time, the accidental mention of pig always bored him, and he could at all times dispense with every thing that brought it to his remembrance. Annabella therefore turned the canvas, and presented the pig-sty to the eyes of Jeremiah. The parent of Thomas felt an involuntary shudder, and was instinctively turning away, when he recollected that the attorney had built no such receptacle in his forest, and he immediately concluded that the whole was a deception. He advanced in a rage towards the pig-sty, seized the canvas in his hand, and discovered behind it the pallid form of Annabella, and overcome by passion, he lifted up his sword to cut off her head!

It happened, fortunately for Annabella, that in the agony of fear, she moved her foot on a button which communicated with a spring, which opened a trap door, on which she was by chance standing. She descended immediately, and on looking up had the pleasure of seeing the sword of Jeremiah fall without injury on the very place where her head had been the moment before! The trap door closed immediately, and being concealed by high grass, could not possibly be discovered, except by those who knew the secret, so very artfully was it contrived. Annabella descended very rapidly in the dark, and at the bottom found herself in the arms of her old enemy, the false Armenian!

CHAPTER XXXV.

THE tempest had raged during the night with immense fury round the cave where Thomas and his ten thousand companions were reposing. Great fragments of rock fell on the outside of the recess, and awakened that hero. Great was his agitation at being deprived, perhaps for ever, of the superhuman Annabella. His friends were alarmed by his horrid cries and shrieks of horror. At times they thought that some of their companions were treacherously killing a pig, part of their store. On approaching the couch of Thomas, they found that hero beating his forehead with what seemed to be a poker!

In order to relieve the reader's anxiety we must inform him that it was not a real poker, but the form of one in cork, covered with black lead. This he always kept by him, to relieve any sudden anxiety by a dab on the forehead. Former experiments had given him an antipathy to real pokers. His friends asked him kindly how they should assist him? "Let

us go to the shore," said Thomas instinctively. The army
dressed themselves, and obeyed him. On the shore billows
were rolling rapidly. Waves like mountains, lowered their
curled heads, and cast the spray on the sands.—At last they
saw something white, riding on the top of a distant wave.
As it drew nearer, the whole army knelt down, thinking it a
tutelary saint; or, at least, the genius of Britain.—Suddenly
the waves threw an inanimate female form upright on the
sands. A Pagan would have imagined it another Venus
rising from the sea. The reader will be surprized to find
that it was Annabella! but the thing is not the less true on
that account. Awhile she stood insensible; at last she gave
a stifled groan. The eyes of the lovers met; they tottered,
fell, and fainted in each other's arms! O, moment of ecstasy!
worth ten thousand years of common life! The army who,
as well as Ergathea, knew what was what, poured a spirituous cordial down their throats, and recovered them. They
led them to elegant and separate couches within the cave,
carefully laying the succedaneous poker of Thomas on his
pillow, that in case of any new agitation he might have
immediate relief. He might be jealous! and, in fact, he had
reason to be so, for all the ten thousand Spaniards were desperately in love with Annabella. In the agony of their feelings, they all placed the hilts of their swords on the ground,
and would have fallen on the points, but, luckily, an army
of thirty thousand Frenchmen appeared in sight. Careless of
life they easily vanquished the foe, and returned in triumph
to the cave. Thus we see the immense service which Annabella rendered to the cause of Spain! Without Thomas, the
affair would never have begun; without Annabella it would
never have ended!—Bless you both!

The troops, warmed by this little skirmish, totally
forgot their intended purpose. On examining into the
damage received, they found that one of their men, who
had advanced too incautiously on the enemy, had received

a severe sabre wound in his little finger. Annabella gracefully bound up the wound; and, as a recompense for their
trouble, kindly suffered the whole of them, man by man,
to kiss her hand. Thomas suffered the pangs of jealousy
to wring his soul; and Annabella, to ease his mind, flew to
him, and tenderly impressed three-and-thirty kisses on the
dear mark on the neck of Thomas! Love conveyed them to
his heart, and reckoned them at forty, so delicious were the
sensations they afforded. The whole army in turn became
jealous, and rushed forwards to kill Thomas, when Annabella drew forth her harp, and elicited such heaven-born
soothing melody, that every man was arrested in the pos-
ture in which he was. She explained to them, on her daedal
instrument, that her heart was for ever devoted to Thomas,
and if that hero were no more, her widowed heart would
weep drops of blood, till the harsh fates should call her to
the tomb. "If," continued she, in the sweetest notes, "you
wish to kiss my hand, or if you have any wish for an old
slipper, to divide among you, as a mark of my regard, you
are perfectly welcome." The army, of course, was instantly
softened, kissed her hand, took the slipper, sheathed their
swords, shook hands with Thomas, and entered the cave to
divide that sweet monument of affection!

The sudden appearance of Annabella on the shore was
occasioned by this. The Armenian had, by nefarious acts,
collected an immense treasure, which he thought he should
enjoy more safely in a foreign land. They sailed as far as the
Spanish coast, when the ship broke. The light form of Annabella, assisted by her dress, and some cork soles which she
happened to wear, floated on the water; but the Armenian,
whose girdle was loaded with gold, sunk to the bottom of
the ocean; from whence it would be worth the while of any
speculating person to fish him up.

CHAPTER XXXVI.

"Will you hear a Spanish Lady,
        How she woo'd an Englishman,
Garments gay, as rich as may be,
    Deck'd with jewels she had on.

Of a comely countenance, and grace was she,
And by birth, and parentage, of high degree."*

THE attractions of Thomas, especially since the adventure of the waxed rope, were so infinitely increased, that
no woman, of whatever age, country, or condition, could
behold that bundle of perfection, without a desire to appro-
priate it to herself. The tenderest lovers, and the most jealous husbands, aware of the impossibility of resisting this
feeling, were not vexed that their mistresses and wives
should entertain a latent preference of Thomas.

It cannot be supposed that these charms lost their effect
on "The Rich Widow of the Mountains," as she was called,
Donna Isabella Fontana. She had long loved Thomas,
from what she had heard of his merit, his beauty, and his
courage.

"Maria," said she, to her attendant, when our hero had
landed in Spain, "my Thomas has come!" "What Thomas?"
asked she. "Thomas, the son of Jeremiah, the descendant
of Alexander, a progeny of a nobleman at the court of
Normandy."

The common reader will be surprised at this Lady's perfect knowledge of Thomas. The fact is, that she was very
intimate with the Queen, who told her what she heard about
Thomas from the Prince of the Peace,* who had it in a letter
written with Buonaparte's own hand. That wily Corsican
often hinted to those he wrote to, and especially to his Gen-
erals, how easy it would be to make Thomas eclipse them

all. Their fear of Thomas prevented them from making any attempt against his power, and had occasioned the length of his reign. The intelligent and political historian who intends to inform posterity of the events of these days, will do well to carry this book about with him, as an easy solution of all possible difficulties, past, present, and to come.

"Maria," said Isabella, "we will disguise ourselves as soldiers, and join the band of Thomas. I shall find some means of gaining that hero's love; or if I fail, I will decoy him from his troops, and confine him in a dungeon till he consents to marry me. Without Thomas life would cease to be life, purple would become scarlet, and green yellow. O Thomas, idol of my soul, light of Isabella!" cried Donna Isabella; at these words she fainted, and Maria, with trembling and unassured step, conveyed her to her couch.

"What is the cause of all this?" asked an old domestic; "Thomas," answered she. "Thomas!" cried he, "Thomas is the cause of every thing; Thomas! I think the whole world is bethomased!"

CHAPTER XXXVII.

THOMAS, whose mind could not rest easy under undischarged obligation, determined to repay Buonaparte for the use of his turtle-tub. Generous mortal! What would he have done if, instead of half a day, he had laid in the turtle-tub half a year? He determined to station persons with speaking trumpets at the passes of the Pyrenees, to inform him that Thomas was in Spain. He also set up boards with this inscription, "Thomas is here;" for his humane soul revolted at the disagreeable necessity of cutting off the usurper's head. "Let him live, poor fellow!" said he to himself, "there is room in the world for both of us." Buonaparte, hearing of this uproar in Spain, marched to the Pyrenees with an overwhelming force. When he arrived there, he heard the name of Thomas resound from hill to hill; on every bush and tree he saw the name of Thomas. "Ha!" cried he to himself, "this is no place for me, my Marshals shall look to it, never more will I in person undertake a foreign war. Thomas will always await me. O, ye recesses of St. Cloud,* hide me from the brand of Thomas!" Thus we see that neither indolence nor uxoriousness keeps him at home, but the fear of Thomas.

Depend upon it, my dear reader, it is of the utmost consequence to know clearly the cause of every event. The fewer causes the better; carry Thomas with you, as an universal solvent, and all will be well. Buonaparte being gone, the poor marshals were delivered over to the fear of Thomas, and a bad life they had. Sometimes he would employ men to steal their bread and butter from them, mix water with their wine, and frighten them in the middle of the night, by springing watchmen's rattles under their windows, insomuch that the poor rogues could neither eat nor sleep, nor drink, nor think, nor act to any purpose.

But to return to Isabella. In the dead of the night, she and Maria dressed themselves in men's attire, and sought the mountains, where that hero Thomas, and his patriot band were concealed. Thomas had passed the night on a neighbouring rock in the contemplation of the comet; for, like Cæsar, he was fond of astronomy.* He was a good astrologer, and was perfectly convinced that it portended himself; and setting down the Great Bear as Buonaparte, he concluded, from the comet's near approach to that constellation, that he should play the bear with that personage. After he should have restored the Spanish monarchy, he doubted, like other heroes, what he should do next—Should he make a total conquest of Africa, with all its lions, crocodiles, mummies, and man-eaters? The easiness of the thing allured him, and, but that his name was sufficiently known, it would give some éclat to be monarch of one quarter of the world. At all events he was certain that if he did not effect this, the world would be convinced that he had no desire to do it. They know Thomas. At some times he sought to scize upon all the islands in the whole world, and by means of an immense navy, to form an insular dominion, with the title of "The Island King."

But when he reflected that he must add to it his own country, the Queen of the Ocean, the last retreat of freedom from that usurper, whose people had so opprobriously taken him for a mermaid; when he thought of the popular government of its aged Sovereign, surrounded as he was with enlightened men, such as Lord L—l, and Mr. ——,* his heart softened, and tears dropped from his eyes, as fast as water from a thawing icicle.

He was in this state of mind, when one of his men shouted out, "Thomas, Thomas!", for he never suffered the addition of Mr., having observed that people on friendly and equal terms very rarely made use of it to each other; that it degraded and estranged the persons always so addressed, and was only proper towards the lowest rank of tradesmen and artificers. These, whether right or wrong, were the ideas of Thomas on the subject, and he has often found himself as if removed a thousand leagues, when in the midst of a friendly and interesting conversation, he has been suddenly addressed by the name "Mr. Bailey." But, to let it pass, the man shouted, "Thomas," and Thomas descended from the rock. He came to inform him that two strange and suspicious characters had come to join the army.

The reader will be surprized to find that these were Isabella and Maria.—"O world! thy slippery tricks!"—*

Thomas having viewed these characters attentively, was convinced of their being spies, and accordingly ordered them to be confined in a dungeon within the cavern, till the bustle of war, and his own ideas, should give him time to

examine them more minutely. The mind of Thomas, liberated from this affair, immediately lost itself in the vortex of
sublimity.

Thus far, Lady Caroline, have I advanced in my story;
too happy if it should have your approbation, which I
should value more than the roar of multitudes.*

CHAPTER XXVIII.

ANNABELLA, whose knowledge in physiognomy could not
be deceived, knew instantly that the two personages locked
up by Thomas were females, and that one of them loved
that hero above every thing. She had often complained
within herself of the apparent neglect of the son of Jeremiah. She thought, mistaken heroine! but heroines are apt
to be jealous, that Thomas, led away by ambition, had forgotten his Annabella. Alas! had that hero held all the world
in one hand, and Annabella in the other, he would have
dropped the world, if obliged to forego one, and would have
retained Annabella. Our heroine, touched with these ideas,
grew sad and gloomy towards Thomas, and the mountains
resounded with the mournful sounds of her harp. She determined to spite Thomas. If he wished to walk out, she would
stay in the cave; and vice versa; if Thomas praised giblets,
Annabella would prefer the goose; if Thomas favoured
goose, she would uncover her harp, and elicit the most
dulcet notes in laud of giblets; if he laughed, she cried; and
if he cried, she laughed. Thomas by degrees imitated her; in
short, if they had been married a couple of years, they could
not have behaved worse to each other. O, Ethelinda, Annabella, Nicholas, Alexander, is it come to this? But calm your
spirits, gentle reader; trust in the author, who, by hook or
by crook, will make all things even: never fear.

Such was the perversity of Annabella, that Thomas

actually thought she had deserted him, and had fallen in love with his army. Under this impression, he gave himself such desperate raps on the forehead with his succedaneous poker, that if the stoutest fly, that ever frequented a butcher's shop, on a market day, had been there, it would have gone hard with him. Thomas concluded that the best way would be to put Annabella to death in bed, to slay the army, make an immense funeral pile, and die like Dido on the top of it.* Maddening with this idea, he seized a sword, and rushed with horrific steps to the chamber of Annabella. How great was his surprize to see another head resting on the same pillow! He was going to strike, when Annabella spoke a few words in her sleep. She cried out in agony, "Thomas has deserted me! O, Peter! O dear Pholy, you alone are left to me!" Thomas, more enraged than ever, lifted his sword to destroy that hated rival, when, observing him more minutely, he beheld a toad. Annabella again cried out in her sleep, "O Thomas, you love me not; ambition has perverted thee." Thomas, convinced of the innocence of Annabella, returned to his room.

Some of our readers may perhaps wonder at the sudden appearance of Peter Pholy; the fact is, he had found his patron, who had taken him to Spain, and when there, he had, somehow or other, reached Annabella. This is the true explanation of an event which, at first sight, might seem a little extraordinary.

CHAPTER XXXIX.

THOMAS was infinitely rejoiced at having escaped the necessity of putting Annabella to death, and quenching for ever the sounds of that harp, whose harshest notes might have calmed the waves of the ocean, and drawn the vulture from his evening prey. In the morning he went to examine his prisoners more minutely, and entering suddenly, he saw one of them with the most beautiful hair hanging down his neck, and kissing with great earnestness and pleasure, the inside of a shoe. On drawing nearer, Thomas saw it was a woman, the most beautiful, excepting one, that he had ever seen. The tenderness of her attitude added infinite grace to her person, and more so when Thomas perceived that the shoe was his own. Aware of his infinite merit, he was not surprized, but he was softened. The tears ran from his eyes like water from the bill of a duck, who has been sifting mud in hopes of catching some ill-fated grub in its serrated border, and in the mildest and meekest tones he blubbered out "Madam." Maria cried out, "we are discovered!" And Isabella, throwing herself in the arms of Thomas, tenderly kissed the face and neck of that hero, thus taking, in one delicious moment, a full compensation for the sorrows of years. Isabella completely lost locality, and devoured with kisses the neck of Thomas: as when the half-famished cat of some elderly single lady, has insinuated herself into the pantry, of perchance a half-pound of butter is found uncovered, licks it with greedy haste, thinking herself the happiest of the feline race, so Isabella.

"Hold your clawing," cried Thomas, in a voice of thunder. "Nay, sweet delicious Thomas," cried she; "I am the richest and fairest of the Spanish fair; love me, and be mine!" "No," said Thomas, "honour forbids me to love but one, and that one is Annabella; were there nothing left of her but her mouth and finger, with which she might awake her harp, and a virgin of Paradise were placed by her side, I would reject the virgin of Paradise, and choose the relics of Annabella." "Then vengeance!" cried Isabella; and, drawing a dagger, she pushed it through the body of Thomas; and then, with Maria, rushed from the cavern, and ran to her chateau in the mountains.

The chariot of the night had long fled away to other

regions; Lucifer had long since hopped on the mountains, and the golden orb of day had long gilded every hill, dale, pebble, and petticoat that lay in his way, when the army, surprized at the long absence of Thomas and Annabella, went respectfully to their apartments, and found that the prisoners were gone, and Thomas lying on the ground, weltering in his blood!

The apartment of Annabella was empty, and in disorder; and Peter Pholy was lying dead on the floor. He had been murdered! as we shall see in another chapter.

The army put Thomas to bed; and then, aware of the generous and patriotic mind of Peter, and in honour of the beneficent and enlightened character of his patron, they buried that personage with military honours, in a neighbouring mountain.

One of the army made a fine madrigal on the occasion, of which the following is an humble translation:

> In honest Peter's humble tomb,
>   Let virgins drop the tender tear;
> Let patriots bring, with silent step,
>   The earliest offerings of the year.
>
> No more the greenhouse thee protects,
>   Or living brooks thy dinner bring;
> Such is thy fate; and such shall be
>   The fate of Emperor, Kesar, King.

CHAPTER XL.

EARLY in the morning, or rather while it was yet night, Annabella had been awakened by the friendly, but cold and clammy blandishments of Peter. She looked up, and to her great astonishment saw four men standing at the four corners of the bed, whom, by their habits, she knew to be familiars of the holy inquisition! One of them, in a solemn tone

of voice, denounced her as guilty of sorcery, and of entertaining an evil spirit in the form of a toad. One of them then
killed Peter Pholy with an instrument of torture! They then
opened the rock, by means of a spring, and then dragged
the screaming Annabella to the dungeons of Seville.

The ill-used frame of Thomas, in the mean time, was
extended on his couch, gasping like a tom-tit, who has been
shot by accident by an unlucky boy, among a crowd of spar-
rows. The army stood round him, trying to ease, heal, and
console him. When the loss of Annabella was told to him,
he fell down fainting, and twitching, and gasping, and howl-
ing for a whole month.

In this time Buonaparte contrived to seize upon Madrid,
Seville, and other places; so that nothing could have been so
unlucky for the cause of Spain, as the illness of Thomas.

By degrees the strength of his constitution got the better
of his wound, and assisted by the army he walked round the
neighbouring mountains. In one of these excursions, two of
the new recruits enticed him behind a tower, on pretence
of telling him a secret. Instantly two hundred cavalry seized
upon Thomas, still weak with his wound, and galloped
away with him to a chateau in the mountains, where they
hid him in a deep and low dungeon! Thomas was entirely
ignorant where he was.

To relieve the anxiety of the reader, we shall inform him
that this was a plot of Donna Isabella; that he was now in
her chateau, and that she was determined that he would
never leave it alive but as her husband. In a few hours an
attendant entered with a light, and politely begging Thomas
to follow her, ushered him into a superb apartment, beyond
which was a bed-room, fitted up in the highest degree of
elegance.

Thomas was in the highest degree of confusion, when
the sudden entrance of Isabella informed him of the dreadful truth! He was now completely in the power of that lady,

who would force him to marry, and he should be for ever ruined. Thomas regarded her with a firmness she did not expect. She informed him that it was her fixed determination to marry him; that she would give him two days to consider the matter, and if, in that time, he was not compliant, she would marry him by force. At these words she left the room. Foreseeing the impossibility, we shall not attempt to describe the sensations of Thomas. All his former situations seemed to him a paradise. He would with transport have been in the glass-house, the turtle-tub, the bottom of the pool, anywhere, in short, but where he was.

Night had now thrown her sable wing over beast and bird, when Thomas, who had been completely agitated, was desirous of repose. He entered his bed-room, but, to his great horror, the fastenings were all on the outside. It now occurred to him to push his bed against the door, and to take a little feverish repose in his clothes; for he was determined, on many accounts, not to undress himself. He secreted a dagger in his pocket, with which he might defend himself in any extremity. The night passed quietly, and the next day. Thomas saw nobody but the attendant who brought his food.

On the following morning, Donna Isabella entered his apartment, attended by Maria, and followed by four and twenty young ladies, splendidly arrayed. Four and twenty young noblemen, dressed for the occasion, ranged themselves behind Thomas, after having thrown over his shoulders a splendid bridal vestment, richly adorned with gold and jewels. They then hurried him to the chapel, where a holy father awaited them. The priest first inquired of Donna Isabella "if she were ready to marry Thomas?" "With all my heart," said she. He then addressed Thomas in a solemn voice: "Thomas, son of Jeremiah, descendant of Alexander, progeny of a Nobleman at the Court of the Duke of Normandy, are you willing to marry Donna Isabella?" "No!"

said Thomas, in a voice of thunder, and dashing the book from the hands of the priest, he ascended to his chamber with the velocity of a mountain torrent.

CHAPTER XVI.

ANNABELLA was stretched on the floor of a dark dungeon, in the house of the inquisition. Her nightly ear was harassed by the sounds of chains, groans, sighs, and exclamations. She had seen her last friend expire under the hand of the tormentor, and she herself racked or burned to death, would fly to other planets, to seek in them a more faithful lover, a more lasting friend.

She endeavoured to paint on her exquisite instrument, her sorrows and her fear, and was filling the building with the softest and most heart-rending strains, when four familiars, whose ears were previously filled with wax, rushed into the dungeon, seized her harp, and threw it out the window.

The fact is, that the Hall of Judgment was directly over the place where Annabella was confined. The Inquisitors, who were sitting in judgment upon some prisoners, felt themselves manifestly softened, and the man who held the rack could not pull it with the proper force. The danger was becoming every instant greater, for who would be able to stop it? If the distant sounds had this effect, what would happen if they should approach the performer? At last one of the Inquisitors, who had read the Odyssey of Homer, recollected a stratagem of Ulysses, on a similar occasion. He went therefore to a distant part of the building, and ordering the ears of the four familiars to be filled with wax, he sent them to execute the barbarous commission above-mentioned.*

This proceeding caused a total cessation of business for

a month, till all the persons belonging to the institution had forgotten the heart-thrilling sounds of the harp of Annabella. At the end of this time she was surrounded by familiars, who clothed her in black, and led her to the Hall of Judgment. There she was solemnly accused of sorcery, and called upon for her defence.

It was in vain that, to their bigoted ears, she gave a full account of Peter Pholy, his Patron, the Greenhouse, and the Millepedes. The reader will be surprized to hear that these narrow-minded persons believed not a word she said. They gravely pronounced that nothing but an evil spirit, in the shape of a toad, could have found a patron, been sheltered in a greenhouse, and have done other things, which Annabella herself had actually seen. They had heard indeed of toad-eaters* having been advanced; but as for toads, the thing was improbable, and, politeness apart, impossible. After a long consultation, the Grand Inquisitor pronounced sentence on Annabella. "We condemn you to be burnt to death at the next auto de fe, and we shall order the civil power to deal with you as mildly as they can. Farewell." The familiars then re-conducted the hapless lover of Thomas to her dungeon, informing her that the auto de fe would take place in about a week!

CHAPTER XLII.

IN the mean time the lover of the dead Ethelinda was in no better a condition. After his tumultuous behaviour in the chapel, nobody had approached his apartment for three days, except to bring him food. On the fourth day he received a letter from Isabella, accompanied with what he thought obscure threats against his honour. His conclusions were correct.

Donna Isabella, though still deeply in love with Thomas,

was so highly irritated against him for his insulting behaviour before the assembled nobility of the neighbourhood, that she determined he should never be the husband of the Lady of the Mountains, at least till he had been sufficiently humiliated.

The ill-fated Thomas passed his days in the most agonizing manner; every foot he heard, every window that creaked in the wind, he imagined to be the step of Donna Isabella, and horror pervaded his soul.

At last the much-dreaded hour arrived, the step of Isabella was actually heard on the stairs; and, to the infinite alarm of Thomas, she entered the room.—"Villain," cried she, "you shall not be my husband, but my love shall not be trifled with." At these words she approached Thomas. At the instant, a secret door was burst open, and four familiars bore the affrighted Thomas to the Hall of Judgment of the Inquisition at Seville. The grand inquisitor asked him "if he confessed his guilt?" "I am not aware of any," answered Thomas boldly. "Did you never appear in another shape than that of a man? recollect yourself." "Never!" cried Thomas. "Not in that of a mermaid?" sneered the inquisitor; "there is heresy somewhere in thus debasing the human form, and as we cannot get the other criminal, it is but just that you should suffer. I condemn you to be burnt, and may the civil power deal gently with you. Farewell."

On the morning of the celebration of the auto de fe, Thomas and Annabella were led to the Great Square. How great was the astonishment of the lovers to behold each other in such a melancholy and never-to-be-forgotten situation! They tottered, and fainted into each other's arms. The civil power then forced them on the pile, and then set fire to it. The united multitude shouted like the host of Satan, and the flames ascended to the heavens!

CHAPTER XLIII.

THIS event would, in all probability, have terminated the mortal career of Thomas and Annabella, but it fortunately happened that an immense mass of people rushed forwards to the pile, and immediately quenched the fire. This was no other than the army of Thomas! They had no thought of meeting with their General and his amiable mistress, but merely thought to rescue two unhappy wretches who they heard had been condemned to the flames.

The reader may easily conceive the shouts that issued from this happy multitude, while they were conducting Thomas and Annabella to the old cavern. Some of the most zealous of them recovered the harp of Annabella; and that heroine, uncovering it in her happiest mood, drew forth such thrilling sounds, that all nature seemed becalmed. Thomas, at intervals, threw in so sonorous and musical a hum, that the multitude leaped about in ecstasy. "Happy, amiable pair," cried they, "live a thousand years!" Thomas seated himself upon a rock, and gracefully waving his hand, addressed the army in these very words: "Spaniards, having set your affairs in order, so that you can go on yourselves, I shall sail to England. I have righted the wronged; and have done and suffered as much as any hero. My name has filled the world, and I wish to make room for another name, perhaps a greater. Lord Wellington shall finish what Thomas has begun. There are some, my friends, who will not believe that I, Thomas, who now address you, ever had any real existence; I forbid* them not, if they will but give the due praise to the recent Ministry, and to Lord Wellington."

The multitude shouted "A Thomas, a Lord L—l, a Mr. ——, a Lord Wellington! May they live ten thousand years! England for ever!"

The hand of Thomas was now joined to the sweet hand of Annabella, by the Chaplain-General of the army. The ship was prepared, the gentlest of breezes wafted it to the shores of England; and Thomas and Annabella long heard in the breeze the grateful shouts of the universal Spanish nation!

FINIS.

NOTES

5 *playhouse at E—*: probably a reference to the New Theatre at Exeter, a thriving playhouse during this period.

5 *Caucasean rock*: The Caucasus Mountains are a range of mountains between the Black Sea and the Caspian Sea. According to Greek mythology, Prometheus was bound to a rock on Mount Caucasus for disobeying Zeus.

7 *venatorial exercitations*: hunting.

10 *The Whole Duty of Man*: a popular devotional book

11 *"What pain it was to die"*: a misquotation from Shakespeare's *Richard III* (1.4.21).

11 *dab*: "to throw or fling down in a rough, careless, untidy manner" (OED).

11 This is the Armenian merchant's first appearance in the novel. The character is a parody of the mysterious Armenian conjuror in Friedrich Schiller's *The Ghost-Seer; or, Apparition-ist* (1789). Schiller's work was first translated into English in 1795 but Ircastrensis likely read Wilhelm Render's 1800 translation, *The Armenian; or, The Ghost Seer*. "He is not what he appears to be," declares one of the characters in reference to the Armenian, "There are few conditions or countries in which he has not worn the mask. No person knows who he is, whence he comes, or whither he goes. Some say he has been for a long time in Egypt, and that he has brought from thence, out of a catacomb, his occult sciences. Here we only know him by the name of the Incomprehensible" (Schiller 86-87).

12 In Lewis's *The Monk*, Matilda gives Ambrosio a magic myrtle branch, which opens any door it touches. Secret springs, trap doors, sliding panels, and trick walls are stock devices of early Gothic fiction and were frequently targeted in contemporary parodies. In *The Hero*, for instance, a ruffian opens a wall by placing his finger on a spider (Bellin de la Liborlière 2: 56).

14 Secret tribunals are often found in Gothic novels of the German school. In *Nightmare Abbey*, Peacock makes fun of German Gothic literature and its influence upon read-

ers when he observes that Scythrop Glowry slept with
Carl Grosse's *Horrid Mysteries* (1796) "under his pillow, and
dreamed of [...] ghastly confederates holding midnight conventions in subterraneous caves" (Peacock 1986: 47).

15   *lictors*: "officer[s] whose functions were to attend upon a magistrate" and "execute sentence of judgement upon offenders"
(OED).

16   *old ruined tower in the neighbourhood*: possibly a reference to
the ruins of Rougemont Castle, in Exeter.

17   *receipt*: a recipe or formula.

19   *breathing gas through a tube*: inhaling nitrous oxide for the
purpose of intoxication. In 1799, Humphry Davy conducted
a series of experiments on the effects of breathing the gas.
Samuel Taylor Coleridge was one of a number of high-pro-
file figures who were involved in the experiments. Davy
published his findings in *Researches Chemical and Philosophical,
Chiefly Concerning Nitrous Oxide* (1800).

20   *comet*: a reference to the Great Comet of 1811, which remained
visible until 1812.

20   *ephialtic sleep*: Ephialtes is the "demon supposed to cause
nightmares" (OED).

23   *pictors*: a play on the word "pictures." Pictor is also the name
of a constellation ("the Painter").

25   *fear, if it rises in the breast of a heroine . . . is more to alarm the
reader than herself*: Radcliffean Gothic in particular depends
upon the reader's close identification with the imperiled
heroine for its effects. Parodies often made fun of the vicari-
ous reading experience that Gothic invited. In *The Hero*, the
romance-reading Mr. Dob is led through a series of mock-
Gothic adventures by his son, Roger. He submits with good
grace to various trials (including spending the night in the
haunted South-West Tower) because he knows that, as the
hero, it is his duty to readers to do so (Bellin de la Liborlière
1: 92).

25   *how well have you taught the female mind to despise all
terrors . . . a walk in the dark from the dining room to the drawing room*: Detractors of Gothic expressed particular concern
over the genre's deleterious effects on young female readers. Critics feared that reading Gothic novels would not only

interfere with the performance of women's daily duties, but
that it might also give young women a romantic view of the
world, which would leave them ill-prepared for the realities
of life. "Are the duties of life so changed," asks the author
of "Terrorist Novel Writing," "that all the instructions necessary for a young person is [sic] to learn to walk at night
upon the battlements of an old castle, to creep hands and
feet along a narrow passage, and meet the devil at the end of
it? [...] Can a young lady be taught nothing more necessary
in life, than to sleep in a dungeon with venomous reptiles,
walk through a ward with assassins, and carry bloody daggers in their [sic] pockets, instead of pin-cushions and needle-
books?" (224-225).

27 *Lady Caroline . . . faults*: an ironic reference to Lady Caroline
    Lamb, whose very public affair with Lord Byron occurred
    in 1812, the same year that the first edition of *Love and Horror*
    was published.

27 *Jubal . . . Amphion . . . Thebes*: According to the Bible, Jubal is
    the father of all musicians (Genesis 4:21). Amphion is a figure
    from Greek mythology who built a wall around Thebes by
    enchanting the stones into place with his magic lyre.

33 One of the defining traits of the Radcliffean heroine is her curi-
    osity about old chests, mouldering manuscripts, and haunted
    chambers. Austen parodies this aspect of the Gothic heroine
    in *Northanger Abbey* when Catherine Morland explores a cabi-
    net in her bedroom at the Abbey, but finds nothing inside
    except an old laundry list.

35 *Paradise Lost*, 2.558, 561 (slightly altered).

36 *Jack Ketch*: the hangman.

37 In *The Anatomy of Melancholy* (1621), Robert Burton praises
    music for its power to cure not only melancholy but other
    diseases as well ("Musicke a Remedy," 2.2.6.3).

37 *defecate*: to refine.

39 *rose of Tifflis*: Tifflis is another name for Tbilisi, the capital of
    Georgia. Roses are native to the region.

39 *diamonds of Golconda*: Golconda was a city in India that was
    legendary for its diamond mines.

39 *Francis Bacon, Lord Verulam . . . nothing remained but the name of
    the title*: Annabella's spurious logic is based on an observation

about Francis Bacon, best known for his theory of inductive reasoning (the scientific method).

39 *Emperor Titus*: Titus Flavius Vespasianus was Roman emperor from 79-81 A.D.

40 Pope's translation of *The Iliad*, 3.364-367. The passage describes the sacrifice to the gods that takes place prior to the duel between Menelaus and Paris.

41 *plains of Ariconium . . . silver-streaming Vaga*: The Ariconium was a Roman settlement in the Wye Valley. The Vaga is the Wye River. This may be an allusion to John Philip's mock-heroic poem *The Splendid Shilling. A Poem, In Imitation of Milton* (1701). Lines 31-32 of Philip's work refer to the place "where *Vaga*'s Stream / Encircles *Ariconium*."

41 *aqua vitæ*: brandy or whisky.

44 *small beer*: "Beer of a weak, poor, or inferior quality" (OED). The reference is to *Henry IV, Part 2*:

> Prince Henry. [...] Doth it not show vilely in me to desire small beer?
> Poins. Why, a prince should not be so loosely studied as to remember so weak a composition.
> Prince Henry. Belike then my appetite was not princely got; for, by my troth, I do now remember the poor creature, small beer. (2.2.5-11)

44 Dryden's translation of Virgil's *Aeneid*, 4.555-561. The lines are uttered by Dido, Queen of Carthage. She foretells her own death and warns Aeneas that her ghost will haunt him for having deserted her. Ircastrensis replaces the name "Dido" with "Tit."

46 "Eloisa to Abelard," line 208.

47 *le vrai n'est pas toujours le vrai-semblable*: the truth is not always probable. "Probability" was one of the standards by which eighteenth- and early-nineteenth-century critics evaluated novels. This passage parodies conventional, and often specious, claims for truth and probability found in novels themselves.

47 *Livy, Herodotus*: Roman historian Titus Livius (59 B.C.–A.D. 17) and Greek historian Herodotus (circa 484 B.C.–A.D. 425).

48 Shakespeare's *Coriolanus*, 2.2.9-11 (a misquotation).

53 *redoubted champion . . . appear at coronations*: Until 1820,

the champion of England (traditionally a member of the Dymoke family) appeared in full armour at coronation banquets in order to challenge anyone who questioned the new sovereign's right to the throne.

55 An altered and condensed version of the *Aeneid*, 1.517-525. The lines describe Acneas's expulsion from Troy.

56 Joseph Addison, *Cato*, 5.1.10

60 According to an article published in *The Mirror of Literature, Amusement, and Instruction* on November 16, 1822, there was a mermaid sighting in Kintyre, Scotland, in 1811, and another at the seaside town of Exmouth, in East Devon, in 1812 ("The Mermaid," 36-37).

61 *in its metaphorical sense, it is more likely to sink a man than to float him*: a reference to the expression "left holding the bag," which means left to take the blame for others

62 *Macbeth*, 4.1.87-89. This passage, which describes the third apparition that appears to Macbeth in the witches' cavern, is invoked as a reference to Napoleon II (b. 1811). At birth, he was given the title King of Rome.

64 "Lycidas," lines 56-60, 62-63. The speaker of the poem laments Lycidas's death by drowning.

66 A misquotation from *Henry V*, Prologue to Act 2, lines 35-39.

68 *so thoroughly club, that Mr. S— W—... would have been delighted*: possibly a reference to the politician Samuel Whitbread, who was a prominent member of a parliamentary reform group called the Whig Club. The floating club may refer to an 1807 political cartoon by James Gillray, "Charon's Boat; or The Ghosts of 'All the Talents' taking their Last Voyage," which depicts Whitbread and other members of the Whig coalition ministry crossing the River Styx in a small boat, using a "Whig club" as a punting pole.

68 *Davy Jones*: "In nautical slang: The spirit of the sea; the sailors' devil" (OED).

68 *wandering Jew*: Variations on the legend of the wandering Jew (a figure doomed to roam the earth until the end of time) are found in many Gothic novels, including *The Monk* and *Caleb Williams*.

69 *Henry V*, Prologue to Act 2, line 42: "Unto Southampton do we shift our scene."

70 Edward Montague's *Legends of a Nunnery* (1807) was one of
    many Catholic-themed Gothic works published in the wake
    of Lewis's *The Monk*. The second title may refer to Francis
    Lathom's popular Gothic novel *The Mysterious Freebooter*
    (1806) or to Horace Walpole's play *The Mysterious Mother*
    (1768). The latter attracted controversy for its depiction of
    incest. Gothic novels were often faulted for their specious
    moral claims or outright immorality.

71 *Paradise Lost*, 1.253. The original line is "A mind not to be
    chang'd by Place or Time." The words are uttered by Satan
    in reference to himself.

72 The mysterious figures are merely servants collecting the
    sheets to be laundered.

74 *Lopez de Vega*: a major Spanish writer (1562-1635).

74 *"breasting the lofty surge"*: *Henry V*, Prologue to Act 3, line 13.

74 In 1808, Charles IV of Spain abdicated in favour of his son
    Ferdinand VII and went into exile with Maria Louisa. Ferdi-
    nand was in turn forced to abdicate in favour of Napoleon's
    brother, Joseph Bonaparte. He was held prisoner for the
    remainder of the Peninsular War.

83 taken from the popular ballad, "The Spanish Lady's Love."

83 *Prince of the Peace*: sobriquet of Manuel de Godoy, the Prime
    Minister of Spain from 1792-97 and 1801-08.

85 Napoleon's headquarters were in the town of Saint-Cloud,
    near Paris.

85 See note to p. 20. A comet was seen in the sky after Caesar's
    death. The apparently portentous event is referred to in *Julius
    Caesar* (2.2.30-31).

86 Lord Liverpool served as British Prime Minister from 1812-
    1827. "Mr. —" is possibly Tory politician George Canning.

86 *"O world! thy slippery tricks!"*: A misquotation from *Coriolanus*.
    The original line is "O world! thy slippery turns" (4.4.12).

87 See note to p. 27. Ircastrensis is poking fun at the convention
    of appealing to a noble patron for favour.

88 In Virgil's *Aeneid*, Dido commits suicide on top of a funeral
    pyre after her lover Aeneas leaves Carthage.

93 Ulysses blocks his shipmates' ears with wax so that they will
    not hear the alluring and fatal song of the Sirens (*Odyssey of
    Homer*, trans. Pope, 12.208-213).

94   *toad-eaters*: individuals who court or flatter others for personal gain.
96   *forbid*: "To defy, challenge" (OED).